"What do you think you're doing?"
Maddie demanded.

"Kissing you. What else?" the handsome stranger replied.

"I caught that." Actually, it had been an awfully nice kiss, but they didn't know each other and it wasn't the sort of thing you did with someone you've never met.

"Say, is the pregnancy putting you on edge?" the man asked.

Maddie's eyes widened. Pregnancy? "Preg… What are you talking about? Never mind. I'm leaving."

"What's gotten into you, Beth?" the man asked, clearly puzzled. "Kane told me about the baby, but he didn't say it was a secret."

Maddie was intrigued despite herself. "It's a secret to me, because my name isn't Beth."

Dear Reader,

My, how time flies! I still remember the excitement of becoming Senior Editor for Silhouette Romance and the thrill of working with these wonderful authors and stories on a regular basis. My duties have recently changed, and I'm going to miss being privileged to read these stories before anyone else. But don't worry, I'll still be reading the published books! I don't think there's anything as reassuring, affirming and altogether delightful as curling up with a bunch of Silhouette Romance novels and dreaming the day away. So know that I'm joining you, even though Mavis Allen will have the pleasure of guiding the line now.

And for this last batch that I'm bringing to you, we've got some terrific stories! Raye Morgan is finishing up her CATCHING THE CROWN series with *Counterfeit Princess* (SR #1672), a fun tale that proves love can conquer all. And Teresa Southwick is just beginning her DESERT BRIDES trilogy about three sheiks who are challenged— and caught!—by American women. Don't miss the first story, *To Catch a Sheik* (SR #1674).

Longtime favorite authors are also back. Julianna Morris brings us *The Right Twin for Him* (SR #1676) and Doreen Roberts delivers *One Bride: Baby Included* (SR #1673). And we've got two authors new to the line—one of whom is new to writing! RITA® Award-winning author Angie Ray's newest book, *You're Marrying Her?*, is a fast-paced funny story about a woman who doesn't like her best friend's fiancée. And Patricia Mae White's first novel is about a guy who wants a little help in appealing to the right woman. Here *Practice Makes Mr. Perfect* (SR #1677).

All the best,

Mary-Theresa Hussey

Mary-Theresa Hussey
Senior Editor

Please address questions and book requests to:
Silhouette Reader Service
U.S.: 3010 Walden Ave., P.O. Box 1325, Buffalo, NY 14269
Canadian: P.O. Box 609, Fort Erie, Ont. L2A 5X3

The Right
Twin for Him

JULIANNA MORRIS

SILHOUETTE *Romance*®
Published by Silhouette Books
America's Publisher of Contemporary Romance

SILHOUETTE BOOKS

ISBN 0-373-19676-8

THE RIGHT TWIN FOR HIM

Copyright © 2003 by Julianna Morris

This edition published by arrangement with Harlequin Books S.A.

® and TM are trademarks of Harlequin Books S.A., used under license.
Trademarks indicated with ® are registered in the United States Patent
and Trademark Office, the Canadian Trade Marks Office and in other
countries.

Visit Silhouette at www.eHarlequin.com

Printed in U.S.A.

Books by Julianna Morris

JULIANNA MORRIS

has an offbeat sense of humor, which frequently gets her into trouble. She is often accused of being curious about everything…her interests ranging from oceanography and photography to traveling, antiquing, walking on the beach and reading science fiction.

Julianna loves cats of all shapes and sizes, and recently she was adopted by a feline companion named Merlin. Like his namesake, Merlin is an alchemist—she says he can transform the house into a disaster area in nothing flat. And since he shares the premises with a writer, it's interesting to note that he's particularly fond of knocking books on the floor.

Julianna happily reports meeting Mr. Right. Together they are working on a new dream of building a shoreline home in the Great Lakes area.

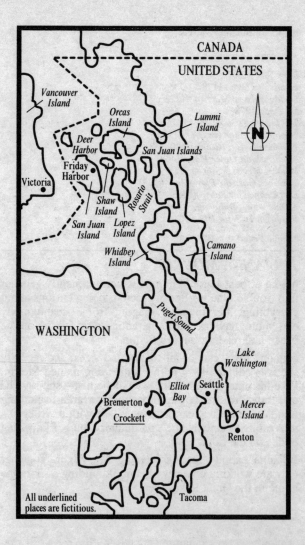

CANADA
UNITED STATES

Vancouver Island

Orcas Island
Lummi Island

Deer Harbor

San Juan Islands

Friday Harbor

Victoria

Shaw Island

Rosario Strait

San Juan Island

Lopez Island

Whidbey Island

Camano Island

Puget Sound

WASHINGTON

Lake Washington

Elliot Bay

Seattle

Bremerton

Mercer Island

Crockett

Renton

All underlined places are fictitious.

Tacoma

Chapter One

Maddie Jackson looked around the friendly town of Crockett, Washington, and smiled, her first real smile in days. She loved it here. People waved from their cars, and the service station attendants had even pumped her gasoline though the sign said it was self-serve.

It was really nice—a bit like her home in New Mexico, but probably greener and cooler in the summertime. And bigger. Crockett had a population of over ten thousand, while Slapshot topped out at seven hundred.

"Hey, kiddo, I've been waiting for you," called a deep voice, and she turned to see a man come striding toward her. He had a loose-limbed, sexy gait and the wide, comfortable shoulders of a football player. At another time in her life she might have been thrilled to see a hunk like that trying to catch her attention.

But not now.

Now she was smarter and wiser. She'd sworn off

romance for good. No more hunks for Maddie Jackson. Not that she had much experience with hunks—only a sort-of hunk—but that was more than enough.

The man stopped in front of her with one eyebrow raised. "Something wrong, gorgeous?"

He dropped a kiss on her cheek, which made Maddie squeak and jump back several feet. Now *that* was new. She couldn't remember an attractive stranger ever calling her gorgeous and kissing her. Granted, she didn't have much experience with that sort of thing, but maybe Crockett wasn't such a nice town, after all. Maybe it was just strange.

"What do you think you're doing?" she demanded, trying to look confidently intimidating.

"Kissing you. What else?"

"I caught that." Actually, it had been an awfully nice kiss, but they didn't know each other and it wasn't the sort of thing you did with someone you've never met.

Maddie glanced around, hoping to see a policeman standing conveniently nearby. Her father had been the county sheriff before getting elected mayor of Slapshot, New Mexico, and she put a lot of faith in law enforcement.

She sighed.

They didn't make men like her dad any longer, the faithful-till-the-day-he-dies sort of guy. She'd found out the hard way, which was why she'd walked out on her own wedding just two days ago. Women tended to do things like that when they found their fiancé in a clinch with the girl hired to serve punch at the reception. Of course, she *had* been looking for Ted to suggest postponing the ceremony, but that was beside the point.

"Say, is the pregnancy putting you on edge?" the man said, and Maddie's eyes widened.

Pregnancy?

This week was getting weirder by the minute, and it had already been pretty weird.

"Preg— What are you talking about?" Maddie demanded. "Never mind. I'm leaving."

She might be shaken by the events of the past few days, and she was certainly a little on the scatterbrained side, but she wasn't stupid. She didn't need an explanation from this attractive-lunatic hunk, she needed to get away from him. Obviously, she wasn't ready to be a world traveler—Washington was a world away from comfortable, dusty little Slapshot.

"What's gotten into you, Beth?" the man asked, clearly puzzled. "Kane told me about the baby, but he didn't say it was a secret. I wanted to congratulate you in person, but the store was closed."

Maddie was intrigued despite herself. "It's a secret to me, because my name isn't Beth."

He leaned closer and peered into her face, the space between his eyes creasing thoughtfully. "I'll be damned. You look just like my sister-in-law. Jeez, you must have thought I was…" His words trailed away and he shook his head.

Suddenly everything became clear to Maddie. It was just a case of mistaken identity—the stranger wasn't a lunatic after all, and the reason that folks had been friendly was because she reminded them of this Beth person. It was disappointing, but she'd weathered far worse disappointments lately, so she wasn't planning to let it get her down.

"I'm really sorry," the man said. "You look a lot like Beth, and since she owns this store, I naturally thought you were her.'' He pointed to the maternity and children's clothing shop in front of them. ''She must have decided not to open today.''

Maddie tucked the information into the back of her mind. She'd come back when the place was open— it might be a clue to finding her birth family. Though, just because you resembled someone, it didn't mean you were related.

''They say everyone has a double,'' she murmured.

Patrick O'Rourke looked at the woman he'd mistaken for his brother's wife and shook his head. At first glance his new sister-in-law and this woman looked identical, but with each passing second he was seeing big differences between them.

The woman's blond hair was lighter and streakier—it looked natural, so it was probably from the sun…and she wore chunky silver jewelry that suited the defiant tilt to her chin. And her gauzy turquoise dress with the long scarlet sash should have been a dead giveaway. Beth tended to dress more quietly, though Patrick had to admit the stranger's choice of scarlet and turquoise was kind of pretty.

''Patrick O'Rourke,'' he said.

''Maddie Jackson,'' she returned, staring at his proffered hand. She finally put her fingers over his, only to instantly yank her arm away. Patrick didn't blame her. The O'Rourke men were tall, and more than once he'd seen a woman take a step backward as if his size intimidated her.

''I didn't mean to frighten you,'' he murmured.

''You didn't.''

Oh, yeah. He believed that. *You bet.*

Maddie lifted her chin a fraction higher and gave her long skirt a tug. ''I'm from Slapshot, New Mexico. And I'm not pregnant." She looked down at her trim tummy, then back at him with a frown. "I don't look pregnant, do I? I mean, I've been upset but I haven't eaten *that* much and I never seem to gain weight, anyhow."

"Certainly not." A grin tugged at his lips. The non sequitur sounded perfectly normal coming from her mouth. "I apologize for the misunderstanding."

"That's okay," she said generously. "You must have wondered why I was so surprised when you kissed me."

Yeah, he'd wondered about that...and he'd wondered why he was having a less-than-platonic response to his sister-in-law. It was a relief to discover the response was to someone he didn't know, rather than the woman his brother had recently married.

"New Mexico, huh? What are you doing so far from home?" he asked, deciding it was a safer subject than the one he'd just been contemplating.

To his surprise, the question transformed the charmingly flustered expression on her face to a blank mask. "I'm visiting," she murmured.

"Visiting?"

"Well, sort of. I was supposed to be on my..." Her voice quavered and she bit down on her lip.

Damn.

Patrick fought panic as Maddie's golden-brown eyes filled with tears. He was lousy with crying women. "That's all right," he assured hastily. "You don't have to tell me."

Maddie sniffed and she made a brave attempt at a smile. "All right. Thank you."

All right?

He was more perplexed than ever. Whenever he

told his sisters they didn't have to tell him what was wrong, they claimed he wasn't "interested" and seemed insulted. Granted, he was a stranger to Maddie, but it still surprised him. The intelligent thing to do was leave before things got more complicated.

"At least let me buy you a cup of coffee," Patrick offered. Obviously, he wasn't smart enough to do the "intelligent" thing. On the other hand, he'd made so many mistakes in his life, what was one more? "We've got great coffee here in Washington. And maybe Beth will show up so you can meet her."

She regarded him for a long moment, then shook her head. "Thanks, but I'm headed for the cemetery. Well, actually to some graves that might be there with my birth name on the headstones. You see, I was adopted and thought I could get some information on my birth family by checking out the markers. Maybe I'll come back another time."

Adopted?

That was interesting. Patrick recalled that his sister-in-law had been raised in foster homes after her adoptive parents split up in a nasty divorce.

"When were you adopted?" he asked.

"I was a month old. My mom and dad are terrific, but I've been wondering about my birth parents—their health history and that sort of thing—in case I decide to have children. Which I'm not going to," she added quickly. "So I'm not actually sure why I'm here. I told you I wasn't pregnant."

Patrick shook his head to clear it. Intimate revelations spilled from Maddie without a second thought. "Er...I remember. You aren't pregnant," he said.

"Well, I was *planning* to get pregnant," Maddie qualified, her innate honesty forcing her into the admission. "But those plans changed abruptly. Thank goodness I found out in time."

"Found out what?"

"Just s-something."

To Maddie's horror, more tears welled up in her eyes. It was so strange being in a place where people didn't know everything about her. She'd grown up in a tiny town, where everyone knew everybody else's business, so what was the point in trying to keep secrets? By now everyone in Slapshot knew about Ted and her failed wedding. Darn it all. Marrying the boy next door had always seemed so natural and expected and now she had no idea of what to do with her life.

"You still seem upset," Patrick said.

He looked uncomfortable, which was fine with her. He'd made her plenty uncomfortable since calling her "gorgeous" and kissing her cheek.

Maddie tightened her mouth.

Boy, was she a dope.

But at least she was smart enough to turn down an invitation from Patrick O'Rourke. He was just the sort of handsome, sophisticated man her father had warned her about before putting her on the airplane in Albuquerque.

All at once Maddie scowled.

Why had her father warned her about other men? She'd told him over and over that she wasn't *ever* dating again and that marriage was absolutely out of the question. She was sorry about the grandchildren thing, but one two-timing skunk was enough.

Patrick touched her arm, concern in his blue eyes. "Are you all right, Miss Jackson?"

She lifted her chin. "I'm just peachy, can't you tell?"

"Uh, sure." But he didn't look convinced, and Maddie tried to relax. Maybe she wasn't going to drink coffee with the man, but that didn't mean she couldn't be pleasant.

"Well, it was nice meeting you." She stuck out her hand. "I hope your sister-in-law has a beautiful baby."

"Thanks."

He grasped her fingers and she shivered. She'd never met someone with his electric body chemistry. The first time they'd shaken hands, the contact had sent tingles clear to her elbow, and this time the tingles reached the bottom of her stomach. It was different and exciting and the last thing she ought to be feeling, especially under the circumstances.

"Uh...bye," Maddie mumbled, pulling free. Trying not to look as if she was rushing, she walked to her rental car and opened the door. She glanced up and saw him still watching her.

She smiled weakly.

Her father had always told her to be careful about strange men. It was the sheriff in him. They might live in a flyspeck town in the middle of New Mexico, but that didn't mean his daughter could take unnecessary risks.

So, what would he say about Patrick O'Rourke?

Something succinct, probably.

Her dad was full of bluster and loud talk, but underneath he was pure teddy bear. Still, teddy bear or not, he'd be really uptight at the idea of a man kissing his little girl who hadn't known her for at least twenty years.

* * *

Patrick stuck his hands in his pockets and watched Maddie Jackson drive down the street, feeling as if he'd just escaped a whirlwind.

Lord, the woman was baffling. And entirely too provocative. He wasn't sure what that business about *thinking* about getting pregnant meant, though it sounded ominously like a romance gone sour. Even if he was interested in a relationship, he certainly wouldn't think of starting one with a woman recovering from a broken heart or wanting a baby.

As usual, the *R* word made him vaguely uneasy.

Relationship.

Patrick shuddered.

It was fine for his brother to get married, and Kane had gotten himself a great wife, but he wasn't about to follow his eldest sibling to the altar. He liked running his radio station and not having to worry about having to get home by a certain time. If he wanted to work all night, then that was his business. Switching KLMS from rock-and-roll oldies to country music had been a risk, but it was starting to pay off. He needed to stay focused on keeping things moving.

"Patrick, what are you doing in Crockett?" The laughing voice made him turn around. "Lately you're always at the station. You haven't even been making it to Sunday dinner with the family."

"Uh…Beth?" he asked, peering at her closely. He wasn't taking any chances after running into Maddie Jackson. Heck, he was lucky not to have been slapped or arrested.

Beth raised her eyebrows. "You were expecting someone else?"

"You'd be surprised," Patrick muttered, giving her a tardy kiss. "I just met a woman who's your spitting image. You wouldn't happen to have a twin sister stashed someplace in New Mexico, would you?''

"I don't think so.''

He hesitated. "The thing is, Maddie mentioned that she was adopted and looking for her birth family. Honestly, you two are so much alike you could be sisters.''

"I suppose it's possible,'' Beth said. "Whenever I've tried to get information about my birth family I haven't gotten anywhere. I'd love to ask her some questions.''

"She went up to the cemetery to do some research. I can ask her to come back if you'd like,'' Patrick offered, at the same time groaning silently. Maddie was entirely too disturbing to his equilibrium.

"That would be great. I'm expecting a shipment at the store, otherwise I'd go myself.''

She smiled, and Patrick was relieved he didn't feel anything except warm affection when he looked at her. His sister-in-law was an attractive woman, but from the beginning he'd realized she belonged with Kane—though it had taken them a while to figure it out for themselves.

"By the way, congratulations on the baby,'' Patrick said. "I'm a little smug about it since I'm the reason you and Kane met each other.''

She beamed. "Kane spent hours on the phone last night, telling everyone from London to Japan. We're going to have a huge phone bill, but he wouldn't get off.''

That was something else Patrick liked about Beth. She was married to one of the richest men alive, but she continued to think like an average person with an average amount of money.

"That's great, kiddo. I'm happy for you."

But the contrast between Beth's bright happiness and the shadows he'd seen in Maddie's eyes made Patrick shift uncomfortably. As hard as he tried, he couldn't stop thinking about it. Okay, so a woman he'd never met had cried twice while talking to him.

It was none of his business.

He was just concerned because Maddie looked like Beth, and since Beth was his sister-in-law, he was confusing family obligations. Except…his response to Maddie Jackson was far too sexual to be confused with *any*thing.

With an effort, Patrick focused on Beth's glowing face. "Okay, you wait for your shipment, and I'll go find Maddie." He kissed her again and watched as she went inside.

All things considered, he couldn't understand how he'd confused the two women. Beth was Beth. Sweet, safe, comfortable. His brother's wife. He liked sweet, safe and comfortable. He'd screwed up enough of his life with things that weren't safe and comfortable.

Down the street was a small grocery shop, with racks of fresh cut flowers in front of it. Patrick ambled over and selected a bouquet of chrysanthemums. It was a small cemetery. He could always say he was putting the flowers on a friend's grave if Maddie got nervous about him following her. He could even say she'd given him the idea.

In the back of his mind Patrick knew he was probably making a mistake to get involved, but it was important to Beth, so he couldn't say no. It was the least he could do after she'd made his brother so happy.

Nodding to himself, Patrick got into his Chevy

Blazer and headed for Crockett's hillside cemetery. The sky had the brilliant blue of an early-fall day and the air was pleasant, with an underlying crisp edge. Soon it would be winter and folks would start complaining about the rain. He'd never understood why people lived in the Pacific Northwest if they disliked the weather so much. Though, as his mother said, being Irish he was genetically disposed to liking rain.

At the cemetery he parked, then used his cell phone to call his brother's private office number. When Kane answered, Patrick described his meeting with Maddie Jackson…leaving out the part about being attracted to her. No sense in complicating things.

"This could be great for Beth," Kane said. "She's always wished she had her own family, especially now with baby coming."

"I know." Patrick looked across the cemetery. In her turquoise dress Maddie was easily recognizable in the distance. She moved from one stone to another, looking at the inscriptions and occasionally writing something on a pad of paper. At each stone she pulled a flower from the bouquet she carried and laid it on the ground. Once the caw-cawing of a crow caught her attention and she looked up, watching it sail across the sky.

He sighed, barely hearing his brother on the other end of the phone. Something about Maddie was so fresh and innocent. Hell, he couldn't remember ever being that innocent.

"Uh…what was that?" he asked into the phone, shaking himself. The last time a woman had distracted him this much was when he was a teenager. He ought to have better sense now that he was the ripe old age of thirty-three. It was crazy. Even if he *was* interested in a long-term relationship, it wouldn't be with a ditzy innocent who probably thought the whole world was like her hometown in New Mexico.

It wasn't.

The world was a hard place, and nobody knew that better than Patrick.

"I'm coming over to meet Maddie, as well," Kane repeated. "I'll notify the helipad and leave in a few minutes."

Despite his inner turmoil, Patrick grinned as he slipped the cell phone into a pocket. Few people had a private helicopter and pilot, always ready to make life more convenient. If his brother wasn't such a great guy he'd be really obnoxious with all that money.

Not that Patrick had always appreciated the way that Kane had tried to fill their father's shoes. Rebellious teenagers sometimes weren't the smartest people in the world, and he'd been a "rebel without a pause," leading with his chin and begging for trouble. A lot had changed since then, except he still tended to lead with his chin.

Carrying his bunch of flowers, Patrick headed toward Maddie. He felt foolish, but putting women and the O'Rourke men together frequently resulted in that emotion.

He cleared his throat when he was ten feet away, and Maddie's head shot up. Her eyes widened and she took a step backward, which made Patrick's own feet freeze. He looked down at the flowers and back at Maddie.

The flowers had been a really stupid idea.

"I realize how this looks," he said slowly.

"No, you don't."

He sighed. "Okay, I don't. It's just that my sister-in-law arrived after you left and was really excited when I told her about you. She wants to be sure you'll come back to meet her." He let the arm holding the flowers fall to one side so the bouquet of yellow and russet mums wouldn't be so obvious. "So, how is the search going?"

Maddie scrunched up her nose and looked at him for another minute, then shrugged, apparently deciding he was harmless. "I found the graves, but they're really old. If these people are my relatives, they're pretty distant."

"It can be tough tracking down birth parents," he said. "What do you know about them?"

She sighed. "Not much, except that my mother's last name was Rousso, and she was really young. My adoptive parents met when Dad was attending the University of Washington. They knew ahead of time they couldn't have kids, so they decided to adopt. It was a private arrangement through a church."

"You seem comfortable about being adopted."

"Why not? I had a great childhood."

"Then why look for your birth parents?"

She gave him an exasperated frown. "I told you."

"You told me you wanted to know about their health history in case you decide to have children." Patrick lifted an eyebrow. "Then you promptly announced you weren't having any kids."

"Oh."

Maddie's teeth sank down on her lip and Patrick regretted ever bringing up the subject. It was somewhere between babies and adoption that she'd started crying the first time.

"Not that I blame you," he said quickly. "Who wants to get tied down with a bunch of rug rats?"

Her eyes narrowed. "I thought you were pleased your sister-in-law is pregnant. Children are wonderful."

Damn it all, he knew better than to get into a discussion about kids with a baby-hungry woman. "Let's go see Beth," he said quickly. "Who knows, maybe you're sisters. She was adopted, too."

Maddie hesitated.

Her first instinct was to say "yes," but her instincts weren't all that great when it came to men, so she needed to think it over. On the other hand, Patrick wasn't asking her for a date, he just wanted to visit his sister-in-law. How much trouble could she get into, especially since she'd already planned to go see the other woman?

Besides, it wasn't her business if the man didn't want a family. She didn't even know why his dedication to bachelordom was so annoying.

"All right," she murmured. "Do you want to go now?"

"Sure. You'd better follow me in your car."

She made a face. "You think I'm going to get lost?"

"We've got a lot of twists and turns around here."

"I'll be fine."

She turned on her heel and headed back up the hill to the parking lot. When she didn't hear footsteps behind her, she looked over her shoulder in time to see Patrick put his bouquet on one of the graves, right next to the flower she'd left.

Her heart skipped a beat.

It was obvious he'd been embarrassed about those

flowers, but instead of throwing them away, he'd left them on someone's long-forgotten grave. Carefully. With respect.

Darn.

She didn't want her pulse jumping over Patrick O'Rourke. Her life had just gotten completely scrambled, and he was completely the wrong sort of guy for her, even if she hadn't sworn off romance.

Right?

Chapter Two

Despite Maddie's assurance that she knew the way back to town, Patrick arrived ahead of her. He got out and leaned against the Blazer as he waited. A few minutes later she drove up, one eyebrow raised in challenge.

He suppressed a smile as she slammed the door closed. "I know a few shortcuts," he said.

Apparently, Maddie couldn't stay annoyed, because she grinned at him. It was the most relaxed she'd seemed since he'd made the mistake of kissing her, and Patrick had time to notice the six small freckles on her nose, which were adorable.

Adorable?

He rolled his eyes and tried to think of something—*anything*—else.

Maddie Jackson was as cute as a baby kitten and had an appealing vulnerability beneath her colorful dress and the defiant tilt of her head. But he wasn't in the market for appealing vulnerability, he kept his socializing to sophisticated women who didn't have any interest beyond the here and now. Besides, his tastes ran to cool, classy brunettes, not impulsive, scatterbrained blondes.

"Are you ready to meet your double?" he asked.

Maddie gulped down a flutter of nervous excitement. She shouldn't expect too much. Patrick was probably wrong and she didn't look that similar to his sister-in-law.

They walked inside the Mom and Kid's Stuff clothing store and Maddie stared at the woman behind the service counter. She swallowed again.

They really *did* look like each other.

"Beth, this is Maddie Jackson," Patrick said. "Maddie, this is Beth O'Rourke."

"Oh, it's like seeing myself in a mirror," the other woman gasped.

"Exactly," he murmured.

Shockwaves rolled through Maddie's already unsettled nerves. First she'd found her fiancé in a clinch with the punch girl, got kissed by a stranger and now...*this.* She felt an irrational desire to move closer to Patrick, as if he was a safe harbor in the middle of chaos.

Beth seemed to recover first, because she smiled and walked forward. "Welcome to Crockett. I understand you're looking for your real mother and father."

"My real mother and father are in New Mexico," Maddie said, automatically sticking out her hand. "I'm just looking for my birth parents."

"I see."

They stood awkwardly until Patrick intervened. "Why don't you start with your birthdays?" he suggested.

"July twentieth," they said simultaneously.

Maddie swallowed and took an involuntary step toward Patrick. She didn't know what she'd thought she would find when she left Slapshot, but it wasn't seeing a woman with her same birth date and eyes and face.

"That's interesting," said a voice from behind them. "You were both born on the same day."

"Kane!" Beth turned, her face transformed at the sight of a tall, dark-haired man with a striking resemblance to Patrick. She threw herself into his open arms.

"That's my brother," Patrick murmured. "You'd think they hadn't seen each other in years, instead of hours. Of course, they've only been married for six weeks, so I guess we can excuse them for getting carried away."

The wry, humorous tone of his voice was lost on Maddie, and her restlessness deepened as the couple shared a lingering kiss. She didn't begrudge them their happiness, but it was hard seeing them at the same time her own life had fallen apart and she didn't know how to fix it. Besides, there was something so...*luminous* about Beth O'Rourke when she looked at her husband.

When was the last time she'd looked at Ted like that? Certainly not the morning she'd found him with the punch girl's D-cup bra hanging from his pocket.

Darn him, anyway. She could accept they'd both been having second thoughts. She could even accept he'd never been unfaithful before. So why did he have to make that comment about neither of them doing any comparison shopping...then make it clear what part of the feminine anatomy he was interested in comparing?

Honestly. She didn't understand why men were so hung up about the female body. It wouldn't matter to her if Patrick was short or tall or anything in between.

All at once Maddie frowned.

Patrick?

No. That was wrong.

Patrick O'Rourke was a temporary acquaintance, even if he did have a nice smile. She didn't have any interest in his body.

At least, not much.

Though she had to admit it was a great body. The kind that inspired fantasies.

"Are you okay?" a quiet voice murmured.

She glanced upward and saw a concerned expression on Patrick's face. Beth and her husband still hadn't come up for air, and a sigh rose from Maddie's chest.

"They really seem to love each other," she said, hating the forlorn tone in her voice.

"I should hope so," he said humorously. "What with them having a baby, and all."

"Yeah."

Patrick groaned silently. He didn't have a clue how to console an upset woman, particularly when he didn't know why she was upset. All he knew was Maddie had that quivery look to her bottom lip again, and it made him feel awful. He came from a family accustomed to physical displays of comfort and affection, so his first thought was to give her a quick hug. On the other hand, his desire to hug Maddie wasn't entirely altruistic; maybe it was smarter to keep his hugs to himself.

Another long moment passed before Beth and Kane could drag their attention away from each other.

"Did I hear right, you both have the same birth date?" Kane asked at last, his arm snugly planted around his wife's waist.

"July twentieth," Maddie said. "It could be just a coincidence."

"But we look so much alike," Beth protested. "I was born at the old Crockett General Hospital at 12:25 a.m. What about you?"

Maddie squirmed. "Uh, same hospital, at 12:35. My birth certificate doesn't say anything about it being a multiple birth."

"Neither does mine, but they reissue the certificate when you're adopted to make it look like you were born to your new parents. Twelve thirty-five? That makes me the eldest. I'll bet we're twins." Beth smiled.

"It's too soon to know that," Maddie said. Judging by the way she lifted her stubborn chin, it didn't look as if she was eager to find a twin sister. "Maybe we're cousins. Cousins can look alike and be born close to each other."

Beth shook her head. "It's too big a coincidence. There *was* talk when I was a kid, but you hear so many wild rumors when you live in foster homes, I stopped paying attention. Wouldn't it have been wonderful to grow up together?"

Maddie didn't say anything for a long moment, but her mouth was set stubbornly. "Twins usually aren't separated when they're adopted. Mom and Dad would have taken both of us, so we can't be sisters."

Realization dawned as Patrick remembered Maddie's firm declaration that her *real* mother and father

were in New Mexico. She obviously loved and re-
spected her adoptive parents; to accept the possibility
of a twin was to accept the Jacksons might have chosen to split them up.

"Hey," he said, lightly tugging a lock of Maddie's
sun-streaked hair. "You mentioned it was a private
adoption. Your birth mother could have decided she
could make two childless families happy by separat-
ing you guys. I bet your parents didn't even know
there *was* another baby."

"Tell us about yourself," Beth urged. "What do
you like to do? Are you married? Do you have children? Kane and I just got married and we're already
starting a family."

Patrick groaned.

Married?

Children?

Both were topics destined to upset Maddie again.
Things were going from bad to worse.

"I'm not married," Maddie said, but her voice
shook. "I was…that is, I *was* going to be, but it
didn't… Oh, dear."

Sure enough, a fat tear rolled down her right cheek.
If Patrick hadn't been so fond of Beth, he would have
glared at her. Never mind that his sister-in-law didn't
know that marriage and kids were sensitive subjects,
she'd upset Maddie again and he was thoroughly put
out about it.

Besides, the last thing he wanted to know were the
details of Maddie's broken romance. She'd probably
talk about it with Beth at some point—if they actually
turned out to be sisters—but he wanted to be miles
away when it happened.

He liked Maddie, he just didn't want to…*like* her.

He'd learned years ago that he wasn't some gallant knight on a snowy-white charger. Hell, he'd gotten into more trouble than the rest of his eight brothers and sisters combined.

"I'm sorry," Beth said, looking equally distressed. "Is there anything I can do?"

Maddie shook her head, grateful for the warmth of Patrick's fingers clasping her own. She wasn't sure how their hands had met, but he had a strong, firm grip. It was comforting. A man ought to have hands that did hard work and had the calluses to prove it.

Boy, was she a dope.

"I'm through with men. That's all," she said hastily, trying to send her thoughts in another direction.

Patrick seemed like a good guy, but it didn't change anything. She was through with both men *and* romance. She'd feel melancholy for a while, which was natural, then she'd get back to normal.

Beth opened her mouth, but whatever she'd planned to say was lost when the door of the shop opened and a woman walked inside, wrestling a baby carriage ahead of her. With an apologetic glance, Beth went to assist the customer, who was casting curious looks from Beth to Maddie and back again.

More customers came into the store, and Beth rushed over to Maddie. "I'm so sorry," she said. "I'll put the Closed sign out and get rid of everyone."

"No." Maddie was secretly grateful for the interruption. Finding a sister was the last thing she'd thought would happen when she left New Mexico— not that it was certain they were sisters, she reminded herself. "Don't do that. I'll come back tomorrow…or call. I'm staying at the Puget Bed and Breakfast Inn just outside of town."

"You could stay with us. We've bought a wonderful old house and it's huge. We're remodeling so
it's a little dusty, but we've got lots of space."

Maddie shifted uncomfortably. Beth might well be
her sister, but she didn't know the O'Rourkes or what
they expected of her. What she *did* know was how
difficult it would be to stay in the same house with
two newlyweds who couldn't keep their hands off
each other. Being a third wheel—on what should have
been her own honeymoon—didn't sound like fun.

Besides, Beth would undoubtedly want to know
more about her almost-a-wedding. She would ask
with the best of intentions, but it was too humiliating.

No.

She couldn't talk about Ted and the way he'd
cheated on her. Not with Beth. It would be easier
confessing to *Patrick* than tell a woman whose husband obviously thought the sun rose and set in her
eyes. Maybe Patrick could help her understand men
better, because right now she didn't have a clue about
the opposite sex.

Oh, yeah, that was a great idea.

Maybe she could ask his opinion about her less-
than-generous bustline. He could tell her if it was really inadequate or just sort of inadequate. Heat
crawled up Maddie's face at the thought. She was
losing her mind—totally bonkers.

"Take it easy," Patrick murmured in her ear.

Maddie realized she was gripping his fingers with
the fierce hold of a drowning woman. With an effort
she let go and shook her head.

"That's kind of you, but I can't," she said to Beth.
"Uh, stay with you. But thanks. I'll call tomorrow."

Beth's face fell with disappointment, Kane seemed

thoughtful, and Maddie deliberately didn't look at Patrick. She backed out of the shop and hurried up the street, her only thought to get away.

This just wasn't her week.

Patrick looked at his sister-in-law's upset face and his brother's worried eyes, and sighed.

He was going to get in deeper with Maddie, he just knew it. Beth was ready to welcome her with open arms, while Kane was concerned about his pregnant wife getting upset. Somebody would have to run interference.

That would teach him to take the afternoon off. Officially he worked Monday through Friday, but lately he'd been at the station seven days a week. Right now he was researching radio transmitters, trying to determine the best way to double KLMS's receiving area. It was a big investment, but it would pay off if he planned right.

"I'll go talk to her," he said, trying not to sound reluctant. He liked Maddie, but getting messed up with her would play hell with his peace of mind.

The reward for his offer was a kiss on the cheek from Beth and an approving nod from his brother.

Well...maybe it wouldn't be so bad.

After all the times Patrick had screwed up, it felt good to be the one helping out.

Maddie's rental was parked at the curb, which meant she was on foot. He spotted a flash of turquoise and scarlet down the street. She hadn't been wearing her jacket and the temperature was dropping, so he checked the rental. Sure enough, it wasn't locked. She'd probably tell him that nobody locked their cars in Slapshot and be surprised to hear she ought to do it here in Washington.

Slapshot.

Who ever heard of a town being called Slapshot? There was a story behind that name, which he'd undoubtedly hear if he spent enough time with Maddie. Deep down Patrick thought the way her tongue ran away with itself was charming. Most of the women he knew were trying so hard to be sophisticated you couldn't tell what they were really thinking.

Patrick pulled a jacket from the front seat. A faint scent of sage rose from the garment, mixed with a sweet fragrance that had to be Maddie's own perfume. He draped the jacket over his arm and headed for her with a long stride.

"Hey, Maddie," he murmured when he'd gotten close enough. "We have to stop meeting like this."

She regarded him gravely, without the slightest suggestion of a smile at his weak joke. "Do you really think Beth is my sister?" she asked.

"Maybe." Actually, he thought it was likely, but since Maddie seemed ambivalent on the subject, he didn't say so.

"She seems nice."

"She is."

"And your brother is really in love with her."

It was the second time she'd said something about love, and Patrick felt as if a lightbulb had gone on over his head. That was the problem. Maddie's heart had been broken. Now she'd met a possible sister who was happily married and newly pregnant. No wonder she didn't want to stay with Kane and Beth.

"Tell you what," he murmured, abandoning his resolve not to have anything to do with Maddie's obviously troubled love life. "If you show me the low-down louse that made you cry, I'll beat him up."

"You…" Maddie stopped and actually smiled. "Would you do that?"

"In a cold second."

Patrick meant it, too. His best defense was to think of Maddie like another sister, and he'd defend his sisters with the last breath in his body. All his brothers felt the same; guys learned not to mess with the O'Rourke women if they had any brains in their heads. Of course, their sisters didn't seem to appreciate the effort and complained every chance they got about them being overprotective Neanderthals.

"Here, it's getting cold." He dropped her jacket around her shoulders.

"Thanks." Maddie caught the lapels together.

"Do you want to get some lunch?"

She shook her head. "Thanks, but not today."

"Come on, Maddie," he wheedled. "It's been hours since breakfast, and I hate eating alone."

Maddie doubted it. Patrick O'Rourke seemed comfortable with himself, though he was hardly a lone-wolf sort of guy. He could probably have all the feminine companionship he wanted, so she ought to be flattered he wanted her companionship. But since she was through with men and romance, she wasn't the least bit flattered.

Well, maybe a *little*.

And her ego was certainly bruised enough to crave some bolstering.

Only, she couldn't. She didn't want to hurt his feelings or anything, but she wasn't…all at once her heart fell to a new low, along with her bruised ego. The invitation didn't have anything to do with her, just the fact she might be related to his sister-in-law.

"Men," she muttered.

"Excuse me?" Patrick said, astonished.

"You're just being nice because I might be Beth's sister."

"Is there anything wrong with that?"

"Well...no, but...no. It's just that things are a little mixed up right now, and I shouldn't be here at all." Maddie sniffed. She wanted to be strong and independent, but a strong and independent person would be home now, dealing with the aftermath of her ruined wedding. At the very least she should have helped her mom put all that food away instead of flying halfway across the country.

"You're not going to cry again, are you?" Patrick asked suspiciously. "Tears make me nervous."

"No kidding."

If there was anything Maddie did know about men, it was that they didn't like to see a woman crying. Her father was a terrible softy when it came to a wobbly mouth and tears, and her mother had explained at an early age that it wasn't right to get things just because she cried.

Problem was, Maddie cried at the drop of a hat. It snowed and she cried, because it was so pretty. A baby kitten standing on unsteady feet turned the waterworks on big time. And she went through boxes of Kleenex at Christmas and Easter.

"I'll try not to upset you any more than necessary," she assured him. "Which won't be a problem at all, because it's not like we're friends, or anything, though you did kiss me. And even if Beth is my sister, I'm not sure that makes you family. I mean, it would in Slapshot because family is family, but I don't know about Washington.''

Patrick groaned.

He'd never met a woman whose emotions were so close to the surface. She blurted out every thought that came into her head, and everything she felt flitted uncensored across her face. Now *he* felt like a jerk for acting as if her tears were an imposition.

"Don't worry about it. Why shouldn't you be here?'' he asked, figuring he should make up for his big mouth, though it probably meant hearing things he'd rather not know about.

"Oh.'' Maddie looked unhappy again. "It's just that I left Mom and Dad to take care of everything. I should have stuck around for a while, then left.''

He shouldn't ask, but he couldn't help himself. "Take care of what?''

She wrinkled her nose. "Two hundred pounds of coleslaw, potato and macaroni salad. Three hundred pounds of cheese, ham, turkey and beef. Over a thousand of those dumb little crusty rolls. Gallons of mayonnaise, fancy mustards and a bunch of other stuff.''

"Really?'' Patrick didn't have the slightest idea what she was talking about.

"Some of the 'other' stuff was a four-tier wedding cake,'' Maddie added, then bit her lip as if she regretted saying anything at all.

He whistled beneath his breath. He'd guessed she was recovering from a bad romance, but he'd never expected something so dramatic. Something had happened on her wedding day? Once again he decided he should keep his mouth shut, but his vocal cords were having a day of glorious freedom.

"What happened?''

"I caught my fiancé kissing the woman we hired to serve the punch."

Patrick winced. Still, it could have been a misunderstanding. "Maybe—"

"Maybe nothing." Maddie scowled and stuck her chin out. "He had her blouse off, and her D-cup bra was hanging from his pocket. What is it with men, anyway? Breasts are breasts. Why does size matter so much?"

Patrick gulped.

He liked women's breasts—big ones, little ones, they were all terrific in his opinion. But it was hardly a discussion they should be having on a public street. At the same time a surge of anger swept over him, anger at the unknown man who'd callously cheated on his bride-to-be. How could that guy take advantage of an innocent like Maddie and still look himself in the mirror? At his worst he'd never taken advantage of a woman, and he certainly wouldn't cheat on his bride-to-be.

"I think your fiancé has the brains of a squirrel," Patrick said. "I could say something about another part of his pea-size anatomy, but I won't since I'm in mixed company."

Maddie giggled, though a bright pink flooded her cheeks. "I'm sorry about that 'men' comment. You really *are* nice."

Nice?

Patrick gave her a measured look. Having watched four sisters go through some unhappy romances, he knew women were vulnerable when their hearts were broken. His sisters always talked about meeting a "nice" man after breaking up with a boyfriend.

If things were different he'd enjoy getting to know

Maddie intimately, as long as she understood it wasn't going to last. But that didn't make him "nice," at least according to the female definition of the word.

"Don't get the wrong idea about me," he said carefully. "I'm not that nice."

Maddie sobered instantly, recognizing a warning when she heard it. Her chin lifted. "Don't worry, I'm not getting any ideas."

"I just don't—"

"I said not to worry." She gave him a tight smile. "But you're right about it getting cold. I think I'll go back to my room at the inn."

Patrick groaned. Oh, yeah, he'd handled that really well.

Chapter Three

"Maddie, wait." Patrick caught her arm and swung her around. "I'm sorry."

She gave him an innocent look. "About what?"

Hell, he was going to pay big-time for his big mouth. "About being a jerk, all right? I've got four sisters and I've seen them get hurt even more when they're...well..."

"On the rebound," she finished, her mouth turned down. "I hate that word, it sounds like something out of a basketball game. But you seem to have forgotten that you're the one who keeps following me. So even if I did have 'ideas,' which I *don't*, it wouldn't be my fault."

"You're right." Patrick held up his hands in surrender. He must have sounded incredibly arrogant, but he'd hate to see a sweet kid like Maddie get hurt again, and he'd hate it worse if he was the one responsible. "If I abjectly apologize and say I was out of my mind, will you forgive me?"

Maddie sighed. She wanted to be furious, but maybe she'd sounded wistful, or admiring, or had indicated in some way to Patrick that she was getting starry-eyed over him. He probably had women falling all over themselves to catch his attention, and she *had* gotten tingles and a racing pulse over him. It didn't mean anything. He was a gorgeous hunk with a body chemistry that could make any woman weak in the knees.

"Maddie?" Patrick prompted.

"It's okay."

It wasn't, but she didn't want to admit it was her ego on the rebound, not her heart. When she'd been growing up, her mother and father had always made her feel beautiful, but now she was left wondering what she actually had to offer a man. Did big breasts *really* matter that much? Maddie glanced down at her not-so-generous bustline and sighed again.

Maybe Ted would have found a kinder way to tell her he didn't want to get married if she hadn't surprised him with the punch girl. He wasn't mean. And if she'd been able to tell him first that she was having second thoughts, they probably would have laughed about it, bypassed the church and had a great party with all that food and cake.

"You don't look okay. You still look upset," Patrick murmured. His eyes were more serious than she'd seen them since they'd met. He put on a good show of being easygoing, but she suspected there was a whole lot more going on beneath his nonchalant exterior than even *he* wanted to admit.

Maddie summoned a smile. "I've had quite a few shocks over the past couple days. I have a reason to be upset. But don't worry about the other thing. I overreacted, that's all.''

"About the 'other thing,' I should explain," he said, a determined expression creeping into his face. "You're so trusting and everything, I didn't want you to start thinking I was some nice guy without ulterior motives. I'm a guy—of course I have ulterior motives. I'm loaded with them. Hell, I didn't put in all that time as a rebellious teenage tough for nothing.''

"Oh, sure, you were a teenage tough. I believe that.'' She made a disbelieving gesture.

"Take my word for it, I was one of the worst.''

Maddie still didn't seem convinced, and Patrick thought about rolling up his sleeve and showing her the gang tattoo he sported on his upper arm. Oh, he'd gotten out of it quickly enough—thanks to a tough old coot whose car he'd tried to steal—but not so fast he didn't have some scars and a broken nose from fighting. Not even his family knew everything about his escapades.

God, he'd been so angry after his father's accident it was a miracle he hadn't gotten himself killed.

But it wasn't any wonder Maddie didn't believe him. The closest thing to a gang in her hometown was probably the crew down at the local hamburger stand. He'd driven through some of the small, off-the-beaten-track towns in New Mexico. They were terrific…and about a million miles from the city.

Oh, but she did have a very sweet mouth.

Reaching out, he traced his forefinger across the fullness of Maddie's bottom lip. Her breath caught and her golden-brown eyes widened, the pupils expanding until nearly all the gold specks disappeared, leaving a ring of velvet brown.

"I'm not nice," Patrick whispered. "If I was, I wouldn't be having so many notions about nibbling on parts of you. But I'm decent enough not to get involved with a woman who wants different things than I do." He dropped his hand before he could be tempted to demonstrate exactly how much touching her appealed to him.

Maddie flicked her tongue against the spot he'd just caressed. He was certain it was an unconscious reaction. Any flirting on her part was almost certainly unintentional: she didn't seem to have a clue about the usual games between a man and woman.

"Different things?"

"Marriage, family, permanence. That isn't me, Maddie."

"It isn't me, either. After what happened with Ted and the punch girl I'm never getting married," she said immediately.

It was Patrick's turn to be skeptical, but he wisely kept from smiling. Maddie might say that now, but she'd change her mind quickly enough. She would meet the right man and forget all about Ted and the punch girl.

A small twinge of pain went through him at the thought. It was the same sort of feeling he'd had watching her at the cemetery, her face turned to the sky. Hell, he'd thought Beth was an innocent, but compared to Maddie, his sister-in-law was a sophisticate. Patrick had never realized it before, but innocence could be very appealing.

He cleared his throat. It wouldn't help to start thinking that way.

"Maddie, I really am sorry."

"Let's not talk about it any longer," she said

quickly. "I don't think I can take any more apologies. You wouldn't believe how many times Ted said *he* was sorry."

Patrick studied the stubborn jut to Maddie's chin; she reminded him of an eight-week-old kitten spitting at a big old tomcat. And as the tomcat in question, he thought it was pretty funny.

And sweet. But if there hadn't been such a gulf between them in experience, then he wouldn't have to be so careful.

"Ted is the fiancé, I take it?"

"*Ex*-fiancé."

"I hope you smashed a cake in his face, or something equally appropriate." Patrick wished he could visit a little frontier justice on "Ted." He might have been a troublemaker as a kid, but the O'Rourke men had always had a strict code when it came to the female half of the human race, and Ted had broken the code.

To his surprise, Maddie giggled. "Not quite. I did throw my engagement ring at him, though. I think it cut his lip."

"Good for you."

"That's what Dad said. He wanted to shoot Ted, but Mom said it wouldn't help, and we were lucky I caught him before the wedding instead of after. And there I was in the middle of it, listening to them and feeling so strange—like it wasn't even me." Maddie bit her lip and looked up. "You probably noticed I tend to cry easily."

Great, another opportunity to say something stupid. That was another thing to be angry with Ted about— if Ted had been a decent guy, then Maddie would have come to Washington as a bride and *he* wouldn't be having so much trouble with foot-in-mouth disease. Married women were strictly off-limits.

"There's nothing wrong with being emotional," he murmured.

"I don't mean to cry. The waterworks just happen," she said matter-of-factly. "But it was funny—after I blew up at Ted I felt frozen. Here I'd grown up expecting we'd get married and have a family, then all at once the whole course of my life was unraveling and I didn't even cry."

"You were in shock."

"I guess." Maddie rubbed the back of her neck. "It was like driving along a road with everything okay one minute and in the next minute the road and signs have all vanished and you don't know what to do. Have you ever felt that way?"

"When my father died," Patrick admitted. "It's a hell of a feeling."

Maddie got very still and solemn. "How old were you?"

"Fourteen—old enough to get in trouble and too young to understand why this terrific guy I worshipped was suddenly gone. I sure got pissed off at the world."

"It must have been hard."

"Like getting a knife in your gut," he muttered.

Patrick thought about the way Keenan O'Rourke had always been there for his wife and children, at the same time working two jobs to keep food on the table and a roof over their heads. How had his father done that?

"So, what do you do in Slapshot?" he asked deliberately.

Maddie gazed at him a moment longer, then lifted

her shoulders, accepting the change in subject. She might be innocent, but she wasn't dumb.

"A little of everything. Mom owns the local newspaper and I answer phones, sell advertising, take orders for the classifieds...whatever needs doing. I'm not necessary, but she likes having me around. Now I have to go right back, and everyone will come in to gossip about the wedding being canceled. It'll be worse than if I'd stayed."

"Why do you have to go back so soon?"

She wrinkled her nose. "I cashed in Ted's airplane ticket to pay for the room at the bed-and-breakfast inn, but the money won't last forever."

"Good for you. I hope he's the one who paid for the tickets."

The corners of her mouth twitched. "He paid for them, but unfortunately we didn't prepay our room reservations. I thought about getting a job here, only I don't have any real skills, and saying you've worked for five years as your mother's gofer isn't impressive on a résumé."

Renewed sympathy went through Patrick. He knew what it was like to worry about a résumé that way. If Kane had his way, the entire family would be working for O'Rourke Industries—at an exorbitant salary. As his sister, Shannon, always said, nepotism didn't bother Kane. He was a great brother, but he had an overprotective streak that wouldn't quit.

Kane had even wanted to buy the radio station or at least invest in it, but it wouldn't have been the same if Patrick hadn't earned it for himself. You had to earn success or it didn't mean anything. He had every intention of going it on his own and proving he didn't need anyone else to get by.

"Tell you what, I'll give you a job," he said, hardly able to believe he was opening his mouth. Having Maddie in such close contact was asking for trouble—it would be bad enough if she ended up spending time with Beth and Kane.

Maddie blinked. "You'll what?"

"Give you a job. I own a radio station. You said you sold advertising for your mom's newspaper, and I'm temporarily short in my ad department. It works out well for both of us."

"You hardly know me."

"That isn't true, you might be Beth's—"

"I know, I might be her sister," Maddie interrupted. "It's nice and I appreciate the thought, but it's hardly a reason to hire me."

"Well, you could save money by staying with Beth. She did offer," he suggested, hoping Maddie would reconsider the invitation from his sister-in-law. It would get him off the hook with the job offer and make his brother's wife very happy.

Maddie shook her head. "Would *you* want to stay with newlyweds?" She didn't have to add *after catching your fiancé cheating three hours before your own wedding?*

Patrick scratched his jaw. He was uncomfortable around newlyweds and he *hadn't* just gotten his heart stomped on by his fiancée. And he didn't know why he was offering Maddie a job. He could claim he was just helping his brother and Beth, but deep down he suspected old-fashioned chivalry was responsible. Maddie wasn't ready to face the scene of her humiliation, and he wanted to help.

He was in big trouble.

If he tried to climb on a white horse and play the

hero he'd get bucked off faster than he could say, "Wounded pride." Hadn't he already screwed up where Maddie was concerned?

Patrick looked at her hurt eyes and surrendered. Something about Maddie reminded him of the old-fashioned values his father had once taught him. He didn't have any choice, he had to help.

"So your option is to go home and face the town gossips, or stay here and sell advertising for a few weeks while we figure out whether you and Beth are related," he murmured, ignoring the warning his survival instincts kept screaming. "I know which option *I'd* prefer, but you'll have to decide for yourself."

Maddie touched her left ring finger with her thumb. She'd worn her engagement ring there for so long it felt funny without the diamond solitaire. She hadn't really liked the single diamond—it stood too high on her finger and constantly caught on things, but it still seemed strange.

Jeez. Everything was so mixed up.

Between Ted and his big-chested punch girl, a possible long-lost sister and that sister's handsome brother-in-law, Maddie didn't know what to do. She needed time to think, but Patrick was waiting for an answer and she didn't want to go back to Slapshot. At least not for a while.

As for the stuff with Patrick and him warning her about getting ideas, she *had* overreacted. Her pride was battered and highly sensitive. She might have laughed at any other time.

"It shouldn't take that long to find out about Beth and me," she said uncertainly.

He gave her a charming smile that made her stupid heart skip some more. "It's hard to say, but you'll want to get to know each other and it'll be easier to do that if you're here in Washington.''

"Okay," Maddie said before she could change her mind. "I'd love to sell ads for your station." She crossed her fingers behind her back, figuring it was just a small white lie. Nobody would be hurt by it, and if she turned out to be lousy at selling radio advertising, then he could fire her.

"Great. You can start tomorrow," he told her. "Got something to write on? I'll give you directions to the station."

She scribbled the information down on the back of an envelope. It wouldn't be so bad, she reasoned. He was an attractive man, but she'd sworn off romance. And even if he *had* talked about nibbling on her, it was obviously something he didn't intend to follow up on doing. Besides, she probably wouldn't even see him that much.

Somehow, that made her feel even more depressed.

"I'll…um, see you tomorrow," she murmured, stuffing the envelope back in her purse.

Maddie headed for her car, still thinking about Patrick O'Rourke's charming smile. She didn't have good sense, that much was obvious. Maybe if she really had a broken heart she'd be immune to the man.

"Drat," she muttered, fumbling with her car key.

"Drat what?"

The voice, so similar to her own, made Maddie's head pop up. "Drat men," she said honestly. "They're nothing but dirty, rotten, cheating trouble."

Beth stepped down from the doorway of her store. Maddie knew her smile was meant to be sympathetic, but the other woman was obviously too happy with her husband to think men were anything but wonderful.

"Want to talk about it?" she asked.

"Not *again*. I...I already spilled the beans with Patrick," Maddie admitted, chagrinned. She didn't know quite how it had happened, but she'd basically told him everything. Except the part about not being completely in love with Ted.

Criminy, she must have sounded pathetic.

She hadn't planned to say those things, but she'd opened up like a chili pepper roasting over a fire. And it was inevitable that Patrick would tell Beth and Kane, so why go over it again? Her and her big mouth.

"Was it so bad talking about it?" Beth murmured. "Sometimes talking helps."

Maddie shrugged. Talking wasn't the problem, embarrassment was the hard part. "Romance is the pits," she muttered.

Beth gathered the lapels of her coat around her throat. "I know it can hurt like nothing else. Several years ago I was engaged to my high school sweetheart. He died in an accident, and I thought I'd never get over it. But I did, then Kane came along and everything changed. I know it doesn't seem like it now, but things get better."

Swell. Not only did Beth have an adoring husband, but another man had been in love with her. Whereas Maddie wasn't sure she'd ever had *one* man love her.

It was worse to lose a fiancé because he died than because he cheated, but if Beth didn't stop trying to comfort her, she might have to scream.

Patrick's Blazer was parked near Maddie's rental, but when he saw Maddie and Beth talking nearby, he veered into a small café.

JULIANNA MORRIS   49

He barely noticed the steaming cup of coffee set in front of him. What was he doing, trying to rescue Maddie? It wasn't that he minded helping her, but he was lousy at the white knight business. Sooner or later he'd mess things up, and that wouldn't help Maddie in the slightest. If she just hadn't looked at him with those big golden-brown eyes, all sweet and hurt, he would have been all right.

When it got right down to it, a man couldn't be responsible for good sense when a woman had eyes like that.

Chapter Four

Based on her mother's advice, Maddie showed up at the KLMS radio station wearing simple gold earrings rather than the more colorful Southwest jewelry she preferred. She'd mostly brought casual clothing to Washington, but she had gotten a black blazer to wear over her dress printed with bright red, green and yellow chili peppers.

"Ms. Jackson?" asked the receptionist. She was a cool brunette with the square jaw of a police sergeant. Still, there was something Maddie liked about her. It was hard *not* to like someone wearing a whimsical, cat-shaped lapel pin with bright green eyes.

"Yes, I'm supposed to start working here today."

The woman nodded, her eyes narrow with disapproval. "You're late. Mr. O'Rourke expected you five minutes ago."

"That's not true," Maddie replied with cheerful honesty. "I'm at least fifteen minutes late. What's your name?"

"Er…Candace Finney."

"Happy to meet you, Candace. I'm Maddie." Maddie stuck out her hand and received a tentative shake. "Has anyone ever called you Candy? You look like a Candy to me."

The beginnings of a shy smile brightened the receptionist's stern face. "My mother used to call me Candy, but no one else."

"Mind if I do?"

"Please. That is, I'd like it. I'll let Mr. O'Rourke know you've arrived," Candy said. She picked up the phone and dialed a number. "Mr. O'Rourke? Yes, Ms. Jackson is here."

A few minutes later Patrick strode out to find Maddie and his receptionist deep in conversation.

Patrick stopped and stared.

Miss Finney—the Formidable Finn as she was called by one and all—was giggling. In all the years Patrick had worked at the station he'd never once seen the Formidable Finn even crack a smile. But Maddie had gotten giggles in under an hour.

Hell, Maddie might actually *be* able to sell advertising, if she could succeed where so many others had failed.

"Mr. O'Rourke, I'm sorry about the time," Miss Finney said when she spotted him. "But Maddie and I have been talking."

Maddie wrinkled her nose and shook her head. "Candy is being nice, but I was late. Are you going to fire me, Patrick?"

He was insane to hire her in the first place, but firing was out of the question. It wasn't just a matter of helping Maddie, it was being there for his brother and Beth, the way Kane had always been there for the rest of the family. Kane deserved to have someone else step up to the plate and take responsibility. There hadn't been many opportunities, and Patrick couldn't miss this one.

"No." Patrick forced a smile. "You're not fired. Come along, and I'll show you the station. Then you can talk to Stephen Traver. He's the head of the advertising and promotions department. He'll be your supervisor."

Actually, *department* was a grand name for two employees who sold radio ads and managed the radio prize giveaways. The business was doing much better since a successful promotion that summer. Patrick had thought of offering a "date with a billionaire" as a prize, with his brother as the billionaire in question. The whole thing ended with Kane marrying the prize-winner—Beth—and the radio station benefiting from the excitement and publicity generated by their romance.

Now Patrick had to keep things moving. People were listening to the station, but it was mostly a fad, and they could stop as quickly as they'd started. It wasn't that he was in competition with Kane, he just wanted to make it on his own. There were too many people who assumed he was sliding through life on his wealthy brother's coattails, and the messes he'd gotten into as a teenager didn't help that image.

"What kind of music do you play here?" Maddie asked as they walked down the hall.

"What kind of..." Patrick stared. "Are you serious?"

She gave him an innocent look. "You never mentioned it when we talked about a job. But I don't

suppose it matters. Selling advertising is mostly talking so fast they don't have time to say no.''

Well, if anyone could talk fast and bewilder a reluctant businessman, it would be Maddie. "We're a
country music station,'' he said as severely as possible. "Do you know anything about country?''

"I'm from Slapshot, New Mexico, what do you
think?''

Patrick didn't have a clue about Slapshot. He had
never even heard of the place before meeting Maddie.
"Do you know anything about country *music?*'' he
repeated with a patience he didn't feel.

Her eyes rolled. "Slapshot is in the Magdalena
Mountains, over two hours from Albuquerque, and
generally considered to be in the middle of nowhere.
The only radio station we get is so 'country' they
won't even play songs with steel guitars in them.''

Somehow, that didn't reassure Patrick. "Sounds
great,'' he lied. "You know all about it, then.''

"Enough. Besides, how much do you have to know
to sell air on the radio? I mean, it's *air.*''

He opened his mouth an instant before he saw the
laughter lurking in Maddie's golden-brown eyes. Apparently, she wasn't quite as dizzy as her runaway
mouth made her sound.

"Has anyone told you what a pill you are?'' Patrick
asked, both amused and irritated. He had as good a
sense of humor as anyone, but the station was important to him. Every penny he owned was invested
in the place.

"Everyone from my parents to my fourth-grade
teacher.''

"*That* I can believe.''

She wrinkled her nose and grinned up at him. Most

people were intimidated by ''the boss,'' but he supposed she didn't have experience with intimidation
since she'd worked for her mother back in Slapshot.
Actually, Maddie probably wasn't intimidated by
anything except a slimeball fiancé who thought her
breasts weren't big enough for him. It must have been
an awful blow to her self-confidence, especially for
such an innocent baby.

Patrick grimaced.

He needed to remember *he* wasn't guilty of hurting
Maddie, it was her scuzzy-almost-a-husband fiancé.

''That's the broadcast booth,'' he murmured as
they walked into the heart of the station. ''We trans-
mit a full twenty-four hours a day, and someone is
always supposed to be in the booth. When you work
for a radio station the most important thing to remember is that there's nothing worse than dead air.''

The producer of the morning show was inside with
the DJ, so Patrick waved and continued walking.

''How did you end up with a radio station?'' Maddie asked. ''Did you start out as a disc jockey?''

''*No.*'' Patrick shuddered at the thought. ''I was
working here, plus two other jobs and saving every
nickel, figuring I'd invest it at the right time. Then I
realized I already knew a lot about radio and liked
the business, so I made a deal with old C. D. Dugan
to buy the station when he retired.''

Patrick didn't add that it was C. D. Dugan who'd
caught him trying to hotwire a truck when he was
fifteen. C.D. had hauled him out by the collar and
shaken him like a naughty puppy. Then he'd made
Patrick work at the station after school in exchange
for not being arrested. It had taken some time, but in
the end C.D. had straightened him out, becoming a

cross between surrogate grandfather and hard-nosed parole officer.

"It looks like you've done a good job here." Maddie's expression seemed wistful, and Patrick sighed.

"What is it?" he asked.

"Nothing."

Yeah, he believed that.

Maddie's face had the look a kid gets with his or her face pressed to a candy shop window.

He stopped and lifted an eyebrow. "Well?"

She sighed. "It's just that I've never figured out what to do with my life. I think that's why it shook me up so much when I found out about Ted and…and broke things off."

Ted.

Patrick scowled at the reminder of Maddie's near-miss disaster of a wedding. The woman was a babe in the woods, and she'd get him into all kinds of problems if he wasn't careful.

"You're better off without him," Patrick declared. "You should be glad you caught him with the punch girl. Staying single is the right idea. I'm all for staying single."

Maddie looked at him curiously. "Marriage isn't that bad. My parents have been happily married for twenty-eight years."

"I thought Ted soured you on the idea of marriage."

"Not altogether, just for me. Of course, I feel sorry for Mom and Dad," she said reflectively. "They really wanted grandkids. And I'd like to have a baby. I love babies."

Patrick drew a deep breath. He'd never gone sky-diving, but he was certain the sensation was identical to what Maddie did to his equilibrium. "I don't want kids," he said hastily.

She gave him an exasperated look. "I know that. And since nobody's asked you to have any, you don't have to keep reminding me about it."

Heat rose under his collar. "Right."

"What is it with you and children, anyway?" she demanded.

"They're okay, it's just that I took care of my younger brothers and sisters often enough to hope I'll never have to change another dirty diaper or read *Mother Goose* again."

"Are you sure that's it?"

"Absolutely."

Maddie's eyes were doubtful, and Patrick shifted uncomfortably. Okay, maybe there was more to it, but it was his business. The truth was, he couldn't be like his dad, not after all the trouble he'd gotten into. His father had been a terrific role model, the most Patrick could ever be was an example of how kids *shouldn't* act. He'd come close to making the kind of mistakes that ruin lives...or end them.

The idea of messing up his own children was more than he could take.

He opened the door of the advertising office, grateful for the distraction. "You'll be working in here. It's small, but it's the best we can do until we expand."

The office really *was* small. There wasn't enough room in any part of the station, but he was building capital so they could expand into a larger market audience. Most of his employees were an understanding group, and the rest didn't say anything for fear of upsetting the Formidable Finn—Candace Finney was the loyal type, even if she did scare people.

Most people, Patrick thought, looking at Maddie from the corner of his eye. Somehow she'd cracked the Formidable Finn's shell as if it were no harder than cracking an egg. Alarming thought, considering the way he felt around Maddie. Of course, he was *much* tougher than Miss Finney.

"Your desk is in here," he said, motioning to a workstation in the corner. The head of the department was just finishing a phone call, and Patrick waited until he'd replaced the receiver. "Stephen, this is Ms. Jackson. She'll be working for you while Jeff is recovering from his surgery."

Maddie smiled and stuck out her hand—back home in Slapshot anyone who didn't shake hands was being plain unfriendly. "Hi, call me Maddie," she said.

She liked Stephen at first sight. He was a handsome man in his early fifties, with strong shoulders and little laugh crinkles at the corners of his eyes. And since Candy had told her—a little longingly—what a nice man he was, Maddie already had ideas about getting them together. Just because she didn't plan to get married herself it didn't mean she couldn't do some matchmaking for other people.

Stephen leaned forward in his wheelchair and clasped her fingers. "You're more than welcome, Maddie. We have plenty to keep you busy."

"I'm looking forward to it," she said, hoping she sounded confident. It was one thing to talk about selling advertising, another to actually do it. Worst of all, she suspected Patrick had only offered her the job because he felt sorry for her. She wrinkled her nose.

Pity was something she could survive very nicely with*out*.

A sudden, unpalatable thought occurred to her and she turned to Patrick. "I need to talk to you for a minute," she announced, grabbing his hand and dragging him from the office.

"Don't tell me—you already want a raise," he said, a smile pulling at his mouth.

"Of course not. I just…you didn't tell anyone about my wedding getting called off, did you? I can't believe I just blurted it out to you, especially after we'd barely met."

Bemused by Maddie's lightning-fast change of mood, Patrick shook his head. "I'm the only one who knows about it here at the station."

"Well, okay."

The vulnerable uncertainty in her eyes made him sigh. He wasn't good with hurt egos or wounded feelings. His sisters likened him to a human steamroller. Of course, they said the same thing about all the O'Rourke men, so maybe the accusation didn't mean that much.

The office door opened and Stephen came out, a thoughtful look on his face. "I hate to interrupt, but I wondered if this—" he tapped the arm of his wheelchair "—was the problem? Some people are uncomfortable about it. I can assure you I manage very well."

Maddie's eyes widened, horrified. It had never occurred to her that her hasty retreat might have been misunderstood. "No. Heck, my uncle has one of those things, and he's the most active guy in Slapshot."

The laugh lines around Stephen's eyes deepened. "Slapshot?"

"It's my hometown in New Mexico. It used to be called Las Damas, but we had a famous hometown hockey player who willed all his money to the town in exchange for changing the name to Slapshot. It's officially called Slapshot Irvine, but we shorten it most of the time. I mean, who wants to live in a town named Slapshot Irvine?"

Patrick made a choking sound, but she ignored him.

"Actually, I was worried Patrick might have told everyone about my wedding-from-hell," she confided. "It was supposed to be a few days ago, but then I found my fiancé in a clinch with the punch girl. It kind of put a damper on the festivities."

"I would think so," Stephen agreed, the corners of his mouth twitching.

"Maddie, I thought you didn't want everyone to know about that," Patrick exclaimed.

"I didn't want *you* to tell them, but it's okay if I decide to," she explained reasonably. "It's not a big secret, just embarrassing."

"I don't think you could keep a secret if your life depended on it," he muttered.

She glared. So she liked to talk and was a tiny bit scatterbrained. It didn't mean she had a problem keeping important things private. Besides, Ted didn't qualify as important, not any longer.

"Be careful," Maddie said sweetly, "or I'll tell how you kissed me before you realized I wasn't your sister-in-law."

Stephen let out a crack of laughter, not the least intimidated by Patrick's scowl. "You're going to do fine here, Maddie. I'm looking forward to us working together.''

Patrick wondered if his face had that deer-caught-in-the-headlights expression. ''I kissed her cheek,'' he growled. ''It was entirely innocent.''

''Did I say it wasn't?'' she asked.

''You…'' Patrick stopped and counted to ten. Lord, having Maddie Jackson around was like have a ton of bricks hanging over your head—you never knew when they were all going to drop.

''Never mind, Patrick,'' Stephen murmured. ''A kiss is nothing compared to some of the stunts you pulled as a kid.''

''Stunts?'' Maddie looked interested. ''What kind of stunts? He called himself a teenage tough, but didn't give details.''

''Never mind,'' Patrick said hastily. ''Why don't you and Stephen talk about what you'll be doing here? He'll have you fill out your employment forms so we can get you on the payroll. I'll come by later to check on things.''

As Patrick reached the end of the hall, he glanced back in time to see a huge grin splitting Stephen's face. If C.D. had become his surrogate grandfather, then Stephen was a surrogate uncle. He'd worked for the station for over twenty-five years and knew more about Patrick's misdeeds than his own mother.

But he wouldn't talk about Patrick behind his back, no matter how hard Maddie tried to worm out the information. When it came right down to it, Candace Finney didn't have the market cornered on loyalty; the entire staff at KLMS was a loyal group.

It was a nice thought, though he should have used the opportunity to warn Maddie about his less-than-stellar past. He didn't think she'd get any ideas about him, but she was on the rebound from that louse of a fiancé, and he was definitely the wrong guy to handle the situation.

After Patrick had turned the corner, Maddie looked at Stephen. "I'm not sure he likes me very much," she said.

A smile tugged at the older man's mouth. "I don't know about that. He hired you, didn't he?"

She lifted her shoulders in a shrug. "He thinks I might be his sister-in-law's twin sister. We look alike and were born on the same day, in the same hospital. And we were both adopted, though Beth ended up in foster homes after her parents divorced."

"It does seem likely you're related."

"Anyway, you'll have to tell me if I'm not doing a good job, because I don't want Patrick keeping me on the payroll if I'm not earning my money."

Stephen rapped his fingers on the arms of his wheelchair. "Why don't you let him worry about that?"

"That's just the trouble. He's also trying to rescue me—which is sweet but hardly necessary—so he probably won't say anything if I'm a complete flop."

Stephen looked thoughtful. "Rescue you?"

"So I wouldn't have to go back so soon and face all the gossips in Slapshot after what happened with my wedding. See? He's trying to fix things so I have more time."

Stephen's smile widened. "There aren't very many people who understand Patrick."

"I don't really, but I'd like to," Maddie said, then realized how wistful she sounded. "I mean, he's an interesting person. He seems so easygoing and all, but..."

"But that isn't all there is to him," Stephen finished.

She heaved a sigh. "No, it isn't. I should have told Patrick I was already having doubts about marrying Ted when I found him with the punch girl. Then he wouldn't have felt sorry for me or think he had to give me a job."

"I doubt it would have made any difference," Stephen said, patting her hand. "And don't worry about the rest. I have a feeling you're just what the boy needs."

"I'm not interested in him *that* way," Maddie denied hastily. "Not romantically or anything. Besides, if Beth turns out to be my sister, then Patrick will sort of be like a brother."

"Right. Sort of like a brother."

She looked at him suspiciously. "Are you laughing at me?"

"Certainly not."

"I don't know why not, everyone else does."

Stephen let out the chuckle he'd obviously been suppressing and motioned toward the office. "Let's get started. I've got an idea that having you around is going to make the day go a lot faster than usual."

Several hours later Maddie was studying the Federal Communication Commission's rules on broadcasting when Patrick stuck his head inside the door.

"Settling in?" he asked casually.

"I'm learning what you can, and can't, say on radio," she murmured, still distracted by the legal mumbo-jumbo she'd been trying to digest. "Stephen thought I should know more about it before I start making pitches to customers. I had no idea there were so many rules about talking.''

''As if you could keep your mouth shut about anything. We'll never be able to put you on the air. Who knows what might come out.''

''Go away.''

Patrick grinned, enjoying the faint pink staining Maddie's cheeks and throat. ''It's lunchtime and I own the station. I can pretty much hang out wherever I want.''

''Well I'm busy, and Stephen isn't here. He said he needed to meet with some clients, but it might have been all my questions that drove him away.''

''He can take care of himself.'' Patrick glanced around, noticing most of the surface space had been cleared of files. Since the ad office was notoriously messy, Maddie had to be responsible for the general cleanup.

''It looks good in here. I haven't seen the tops of these desks in years.''

She shrugged and tucked a strand of hair behind her ear. ''Stephen said to do whatever I wanted. I'm not done yet.''

Patrick looked around again, realizing one reason the room looked bigger was that the furniture had been rearranged. Maddie might be ditsy, but she was a hard worker. ''Who moved the desks and bookshelves?''

''Me.''

''*Maddie,*'' he exclaimed, horrified. ''You could have hurt yourself. Why didn't you call me?''

Her eyelids swept down, concealing her expression. ''I'm not helpless. I just pulled and nudged things around to where I wanted them. The loose papers and files and stuff are in boxes in the closet—I'll sort it out later.''

Boxes? This was going from bad to worse as far as Patrick was concerned. ''Would your father have let you do all that heavy work?'' he demanded.

''No, but Dad is old-fashioned.''

''So am I.'' It occurred to Patrick that he wasn't being politically correct, but the idea of Maddie trying to strong-arm those heavy old desks appalled him. ''Don't do anything like that again.''

''You hired me to do a job.''

''I hired you to work on promotions and sell advertising, not to be a furniture mover!''

Maddie just blinked at him, a tangle of emotions in her golden-brown eyes. He didn't have a clue what might be going on inside her active brain. For someone who didn't seem to have brakes on her tongue, she could be damned incomprehensible.

''And if you get hurt, Beth and Kane will never forgive me,'' he added lamely.

She was silent a moment longer, then drew a deep breath. ''Beth called me last night,'' she said. ''We talked for a long time. She doesn't remember her adoptive parents—I guess adopting a baby was their last-ditch effort to stay together. The judge eventually decided neither one of them were fit parents and put her in foster care.''

Patrick nodded and sat on the corner of Stephen's desk. ''It's tough growing up without a real family. She's thrilled to find a sister.''

''A possible sister,'' Maddie amended. ''I...I also called Mom and Dad and told them about Beth. They were pretty upset about her ending up in foster homes—they would have loved having us both.''

An ache rose in Patrick's chest. Maddie was so hurt by her fiancé's betrayal, and now she was worried about her parents and how they felt about her finding a twin sister. One complication upon another, life going out of control, making it that much harder to deal with.

He knew how it felt.

All those years ago, after losing his father, he'd been out of control. He hated the feeling—the rush of emotions, all conflicting with one another, pain and sorrow, guilt, the uncertainty of not knowing what was going to happen next. He'd left it behind along with the anger over his father's death. Life had been too complicated, too confusing, too *painful* the other way, so he'd worked hard at making it simple.

He didn't *want* it to get complicated again.

Yet even as Patrick affirmed his resolve, he sensed the ground moving beneath his feet, the first real stirrings of upheaval in years. And his father's voice, long suppressed, murmured into his ear, urging him to stop sitting on the sidelines.

''I'm not,'' he muttered.

''Not what?'' Maddie asked,

''Nothing. I just…nothing.'' He shook his head to clear it. Keenan O'Rourke was gone, killed in a freak accident, and if his children sometimes heard his voice, it was only in memory. ''Adoption records are sealed, but Kane's people are experts in finding things out. I'm sure they'll get something soon.''

He would let his brother and sister-in-law broach the subject of genetic tests. Not that they weren't convinced that Maddie was Beth's sister, but it might take more evidence for her to accept it.

"You know, I'm hungry. Let's grab some lunch," he said, wanting to erase her melancholy expression.

"I don't want to be treated any differently from your other employees," she said.

Patrick started to point out that Maddie wasn't like his other employees, then stopped. He could already see the mulish set to her jaw.

"You need to get a feel for the Northwest to do your job," he said. "I planned to drive you around earlier, but time got away from me."

When she remained silent he stood up.

"Come on, Maddie. If you keep turning me down this way, I'm going to get a complex. I'm hungry, and you must be, so let's get moving."

Maddie pushed the FCC rule book away with one finger. She'd been too edgy about starting a new job to eat breakfast, so lunch sounded wonderful. But she wasn't supposed to be spending time with Patrick, she was supposed to be figuring out what to do with her life. Wasn't that the reason she'd come to Washington?

"Okay, but I'll buy," she said, standing up. She could figure things out better on a full stomach.

Patrick glared. "I don't invite a woman to lunch and let her pay. My daddy would have used a shillelagh on my behind for doing something like that."

"What's a shillelagh?"

"A big Irish stick. I'm paying, and that's that."

"That's just as old-fashioned as saying I shouldn't move the furniture."

"Too damned bad."

He had the same old-fashioned values Maddie had

grown up with, but she wasn't going to admit it. "You're going to be unreasonable about everything, aren't you?" she asked, trying to match his glare with one of her own.

"You bet. I own this station, and don't you forget it."

She wondered what he'd do if she saluted him. No matter what Patrick said, she wasn't a regular employee, and he wasn't treating her like one. A part of her didn't mind, but another part wanted to be strong, an independent woman standing on her own two feet. If nothing else, her parents deserved a daughter capable of managing her own life.

"Would it help if I said it's my policy to take all new KLMS employees to lunch?" Patrick asked.

"Since when?"

He grinned. "Since I said so. Let's get going, they have a Marionberry milkshake at the café you can't miss. That's sort of like blackberry, only better."

"Make mine chocolate," Maddie muttered rebelliously.

"God save me from contrary women. For once I'd like to meet one who doesn't argue everything with me."

"I'm sure contrary women are not a big problem in your life," she said as severely as possible.

"You'd be surprised. Give me an amenable guy like Stephen Traver. Stephen would never refuse to eat lunch with me."

Maddie rolled her eyes as she followed him to his Chevy Blazer. "I like Stephen," she said. "Candy told me he was really nice."

"How did you get permission to call her Candy?" Patrick asked. "I've known the Formidable Finn since I was fifteen and never dared call her anything but Miss Finney.''

''Did you ever ask?''

The question brought Patrick up short. He'd been awed by the Formidable Finn from their first, not-so-auspicious meeting. He met Maddie's gaze and sighed.

''No.''

''That's all I did. I asked and she said yes.''

Somehow he doubted it was as easy as that. Something about Maddie was contagious. Her smile, the way she stuck out her hand to shake. She was straightforward and sincere, with a sun-bright smile and eyes as warm as tiger's-eye topaz. Something about her turned him inside out, and that was a problem he still didn't know how to handle.

Chapter Five

Patrick held the door of the Blazer for Maddie, trying not to notice the tiny freckles on her nose and the way they made her skin seem even creamier by contrast.

"Thank you," she murmured.

At least she didn't object to men holding doors for her. He'd run into a few feminists who'd been vocal about holding their *own* doors, thank you.

Of course, Maddie probably wasn't finished arguing about who was paying for lunch. Patrick shrugged and headed for his favorite lunch spot; he'd deal with that when the time came.

Maddie's face brightened when she saw the small café. "This looks like the one we have back home."

"Grab any seat," called the waitress from across the room.

He nodded and directed Maddie to a corner booth. They'd lived in Crockett for a while when he was a boy, and nothing had changed at the café since then—

same food, same blue gingham curtains, same every-thing. They even had the same waitress, though she was grayer and rounder than before.

"I love the food here," he murmured. "It's loaded with all the great stuff nutritionists keep saying we shouldn't eat."

A smile tugged at Maddie's mouth. "Is that so?"

"Oh, yeah. Fried everything with tons of salt."

"How're you doing, Patrick?" the waitress asked as she made her way over to their table.

"Not bad. Shirley, this is Maddie Jackson. We think she might be Beth's twin sister."

Shirley peered closely at Maddie and shook her head. "If that isn't something. Like two peas in a pod."

"Does everyone around here know everyone else?" Maddie asked, blinking. She was used to peo-ple knowing her; Slapshot wasn't that big and her father was the town mayor. But Crockett was much larger than her hometown.

"Oh, everyone around here knows the O'Rourkes," Shirley said as she pulled a pencil from behind her ear. "They practically saved Crockett when they built the textile mill. What'll you have?"

Maddie pointed to the wonder burger meal on the menu. "That looks good. And I'll have a chocolate shake, a side of coleslaw, and the Marionberry pie for dessert."

Shirley examined Maddie over the rim of her glasses. "You're a little thing. Are you sure you don't want something smaller? A meal like that would pack five pounds onto my hips."

"I don't gain weight easily. Must be life's com-pensation for making me flat-chested," Maddie said.

She made it sound like a joke, but Patrick knew it wasn't. He couldn't say anything, not in the restaurant. He wasn't even certain he *should* say something, he might make things worse rather than better.

Tarnation. He didn't want to be responsible for other people's feelings and worry about them getting hurt. But here he was, trying to be a damned hero and getting involved with Maddie in the process.

"All right, then. The usual, Patrick?" Shirley prompted, startling him from less comfortable thoughts.

"Uh, yeah." He handed her the menus.

"And I want the check," Maddie added.

"No, she doesn't," he said.

"Yes, I do."

Shirley hesitated. "Patrick really wants to take care of this one. You can take the next one." She patted Maddie's hand and hurried back to the kitchen.

"You knew she going to say something like that," Maddie accused.

Patrick shrugged, keeping a smile from his face with an effort. Shirley's husband worked for the mill, so her allegiance was firmly in the O'Rourke camp.

It was after the lunch rush, so they didn't have to wait long for their food. The "wonder" burger was the café's biggest platter, served up with a mountain of cheddar fries. Maddie reached for the jalapeño Tabasco sauce and shook a generous amount over the fries.

"Want some?" she asked, holding out the bottle.

"Not a chance. Do you have an asbestos mouth?"

"Nope, but I grew up on New Mexico chilies. We pour green chili sauce over everything that sits still for it." She popped a forkful of fries into her mouth and chewed.

Patrick shuddered. He was the first to admit his diet wasn't the healthiest—mostly steak and salad—but he couldn't imagine eating liquid fire with such abandon. He also couldn't imagine any woman he knew ordering such a big meal when they were out with a man. One of his dates had actually ordered a dinner salad as her meal. A dinner salad!

Christina was a stock analyst—a sleek brunette who didn't want commitment any more than he did. He hadn't seen her in a while. It was hard having a social life when you were building a radio empire.

As they left the café, his cell phone rang and the display showed his mother's number. His sixth sense said she was calling about more than him missing the last five Sunday dinners with the family, and he groaned. Didn't he have enough problems dealing with Maddie without adding family on top of it?

"Is something wrong?" Maddie asked, fastening her seat belt.

"I have a feeling trouble is calling."

"Then don't answer."

He just shook his head and pressed the button. Not answering a call from his mother was the same as refusing a call from the president—you didn't consider it an option.

"Hi, Mom."

"I understand you have a new employee," Pegeen said. She'd immigrated from Ireland as a young bride, and she still retained a soft Irish brogue. "I hear Maddie's the image of our darlin' Beth."

News traveled at the speed of light in the O'Rourke family.

"She's...yeah, they look alike." Patrick cast a glance at Maddie in her brightly printed dress. She'd abandoned her black blazer and looked more like herself. He grinned wryly—he didn't have a clue what Maddie was really like, but he'd bet that a sober black blazer was out of character.

"I hoped we could have dinner here tonight to meet Maddie. Since you'll be the one knowin' her best, I thought you might speak to her about coming, then bring her along," his mother said, dropping the verbal bomb he'd been expecting to hear.

"Mom—"

"Beth says the dear girl is heartsore. We know how it is, after what happened to our Kathleen."

Kathleen.

A hard knot twisted Patrick's stomach before he willed it away. His sister was all right, and she was probably better off without her skunk of a husband, anyway. And if he tried really hard, he could even forget the way she'd cried after Frank walked out, despair and anger and regret all rolled into a gut-wrenching whole.

"No doubt Maddie needs family to help her through a hard time," Pegeen continued.

"We're not...*that*." Patrick cast another glance at Maddie. She was looking out the window with polite disinterest, but she couldn't help hearing his side of the conversation, so he didn't want to come right out and say she wasn't family.

"Patrick Finnegan O'Rourke, Maddie is Beth's sister. That child is as much a part of our family as anyone else."

Using his full name meant he was in deep trouble, and Patrick dropped his head back against the seat.

When Pegeen declared someone a member of the family, then come hell or high water, they were part of the family. Maddie was almost certainly Beth's sister, and that was enough to declare an all-out assembly of the O'Rourkes as a show of support.

This was even worse than his mother calling to ask if everything was "all right." She didn't use guilt deliberately, he just *felt* guilty because staying away from family gatherings worried her, and he didn't have a good excuse beyond work. Kane used to be the workaholic, not him.

Funny, now that Kane had gotten married it seemed as if they were trading places. But once he'd finished researching a new transmitter and deciding how to best expand the station, things would ease up.

"I'll try and see what I can do," he muttered into the phone. "About tonight."

"That's fine, dear. Dinner is at six, but come early so we can visit."

He opened his mouth to remind her he'd just promised to *try,* but she disconnected before he got the words out.

Sighing, Patrick started the Blazer and pulled out on the road. He could imagine Maddie's response when he told her they'd have to leave work early to have dinner at his mother's house. She already had her hackles up, wanting to be treated like "any other employee." Lunch was one thing, dinner with the family was an entirely different proposition.

"It seems we have a command performance tonight at my mother's house," he admitted after a long moment.

"What?"

"My mother has invited us to dinner, and I'm expected to make sure you get there safely. We'll need to leave in an hour to beat rush hour traffic." Maybe she wouldn't notice she hadn't accepted the invitation.

Maddie shook her head with predictable vigor. "I don't think that's a good idea."

"You'll never figure out the Bremerton ferry and city traffic on your own," he said reasonably. "Mom lives on the other side of Seattle."

"I'm not leaving early. You hired me to do a job, and that's what I'm going to do."

Lord.

Up ahead there was a small area wide enough to park in Puget Sound, and Patrick turned into it, his jaw set. At this rate they'd never make it back to the office, much less to dinner with his mother and brothers and sisters.

"Mom wants you to know that you're part of the family and can count on us for...for anything," he said. "Beth told her that you've had a rough time recently and she's worried about you."

"How can she be worried? We've never met."

"That doesn't matter to Mom." He wondered if he should tell Maddie about Kathleen, then decided it was his sister's place to explain.

"Mmm. Beth says your mother is wonderful."

A pleased warmth crept through Patrick. "We're just as crazy about Beth," he murmured. "She's been great for Kane. He's finally making a life for himself outside of the business."

"At least you approve of your brother having a wife."

"We're not going to start that again, are we?"

"I'm not sure we've ever..." Maddie's voice

trailed and he looked at her in time to see a strained expression in her eyes. Her teeth were gnawing at her bottom lip in apparent indecision, and her fingers were clenched so hard on the seat belt strap that her knuckles showed white.

"Maddie, what is it?"

For a moment Maddie watched the seagulls reeling over the choppy water of Puget Sound. She'd been struggling with her conscience all morning, feeling confused and trying to figure out exactly what hurt so much about her failed wedding plans. But no matter how she looked at things, she ought to have told Patrick the truth from the beginning, even if it did make her look ridiculous.

She cleared her throat. "Your mother won't…that is, she needn't worry…about me."

"Moms are genetically programmed to worry. Isn't your mother the same?"

"Yes."

Maddie smiled faintly. *Genetically programmed to worry*—her father would love that description, though she could apply it to him, as well. From what she could see, fathers worried just as much as mothers. Sometimes more, because fathers knew exactly the way boys—and men—thought.

"The thing is, I'm not exactly brokenhearted about my wedding getting cancelled," she said after a moment. "The way it happened was awful, but it's kind of okay that it got called off."

Patrick's eyebrows shot halfway up his forehead. "Oh?"

Darn. It was hard to admit being such a fool. She was reasonably intelligent and should have figured things out *before* hiring a caterer and booking the church. In a way, she was as much at fault for the fiasco as Ted.

Mortified, Maddie climbed out and crossed her arms over her stomach as she stared at the inlet. There was a taste of salt in the air, and ripples of water in Puget Sound were being driven sideways by the brisk wind. She shivered. It seemed colder in Washington than back home, but the fresh air felt good on her hot face.

The driver's door slammed shut and Patrick came around to lean on the fender next to her.

"Okay," he said after a moment. "You don't have a broken heart. That part's good. What happened?"

"I was having second thoughts," she whispered. "That's why I went looking for Ted. We were high school sweethearts, but it never occurred to us we might have fallen out of love, especially with everyone assuming we'd get married one day. I was just as bad as everyone else. I mean, aren't you *supposed* to marry the boy next door?"

Patrick looked thoughtful. "What changed on the day of the wedding? It seems like a big step, especially considering you were planning to get pregnant right away."

Maddie shrugged. "I'd been having doubts for weeks, but I thought it was just cold feet. I should have realized what was going on when we were both willing to wait so long, but Ted was working and driving into Albuquerque three nights a week to take classes for his degree. I thought I was being supportive."

"How long is long?"

She squirmed. "Since high school, but it was never really formal because my father said he didn't want me getting married until I was at least twenty-two. Now I'm twenty-six and still not married. And won't ever be," she added hastily.

Patrick laughed. "Give it time. You'll change your mind."

"You haven't."

"I'm a guy. Things are different for guys."

She rolled her eyes. "So, anyway, you don't need to worry about me or anything else. I wasn't really in love, and I don't need rescuing, which means it's okay if you want to fire me. I'll understand."

Patrick fought the urge to grab Maddie and kiss her generous mouth. Hellfire, he didn't care that she hadn't loved the louse. It didn't make her any less hurt or confused or vulnerable, it just showed good taste on her part.

"Is it any less embarrassing to go back to face the gossips than if you'd truly been in love?" he asked. "And does finding Ted with another woman hurt any less because of it?"

She shook her head.

"Then stop telling me not to worry. The O'Rourkes are professional worriers and I'll worry if I want to." Patrick knew he sounded belligerent, and getting more involved with Maddie was a big mistake on his part, but he wasn't buying her brave talk.

"Well, it probably would have worked out all right if it hadn't been for that punch girl." Maddie scowled. "We should have never hired someone from out of town, but there isn't a caterer in Slapshot."

"I don't think you can blame the punch girl for Ted being a louse."

"No, just my flat chest," Maddie retorted.

Patrick turned and rested his hip against the Blazer.

A lock of Maddie's long hair blew across his shoulder and he reached up, smoothing it back against her cheek. It was pretty in the sunlight, with glints of gold and red, catching on his rough fingers like spun silk.

"Stop saying that. You don't have a flat chest," he said. "It happens to be a very nice chest."

"That's not what Ted—"

"I don't *care* what Ted said," Patrick interrupted harshly. He already wanted to grind the little toad beneath his heel, and hearing more of what Ted had said about Maddie's chest wasn't going to relieve that desire. "And nothing justifies him saying something mean."

"He was just being honest."

"Like hell."

Patrick deliberately planted his hands on either side of Maddie, caging her between him and the vehicle. They were on a little-used back road, shielded on either side by tall mounds of blackberry vines and the tinted windows of the Blazer. It was secluded enough to offer privacy, and public enough to keep him from getting carried away.

"Maddie, he was trying to push his inadequacy onto you. Not every man requires an exaggerated version of womanhood to get his jollies. Some of us even enjoy a figure built on more elegant lines. Like yours. So don't tar us all with the same damned brush."

"But I'm not very generous up—"

Patrick gave up and fastened his mouth over hers. Quite possibly it was the only way to get Maddie to be quiet, and right now he needed her to be quiet.

He needed…oh, hell, he needed something he shouldn't need.

For a fraction of a second Maddie was frozen in

shock. She might have wondered what kissing Patrick O'Rourke would be like, but she'd never expected to find out. One thing was certain, there wasn't a single easygoing thing about his kiss—it was pure electricity.

Maddie raised her arms around Patrick's neck and held on for dear life. Heat poured through her veins, making her aware of every part of her body. The sensations seemed so strange and unexpected, shivering through her body with a power that reminded her of lightning over the desert.

"That's it…yes," Patrick muttered into her mouth.

His hands moved, stroking her back, his fingers gliding over the curve of her bottom. It made her insides jump in response and she stretched more fully against him, feeling small and fragile and protected within his embrace, though she wasn't the least bit small and fragile and didn't need protection.

Patrick was a tall man, equal in size to his older brother, and so similar in appearance to Kane O'Rourke it was uncanny. She couldn't imagine wanting Kane touching her, but she'd wanted Patrick's kiss, maybe even from the beginning when he'd mistakenly bussed her cheek and shocked the socks off her.

Fool, a voice whispered in her head.

Getting tangled up with another man was not the way to discover what to do with her life, but it felt so good having his hard length pressed against her, she couldn't stop. In five minutes, perhaps, but not now. She might be a fool, but she'd missed so much in her twenty-six years that she wasn't going to miss *this.*

The sound of the breeze and the lapping of water

blended with the roar of blood in her ears. Patrick's lips trailed down her cheek and pressed to the side of her throat. He was lightly sucking the skin and she wondered if she'd have a mark there when he finished—something that branded her, however temporarily, as belonging to Patrick O'Rourke.

The thought didn't displease her as much as it should have. She didn't belong to him, and wasn't likely to in the future. The man she kept glimpsing below Patrick's charming, easygoing surface was as appealing as he was unattainable. Whatever demons drove him, they weren't the ones he told the world...they probably weren't even the ones he told himself.

If she hadn't been able to understand Ted, how could she possibly understand a man who was a thousand times more complicated? And she...a sigh escaped as Patrick began flicking her skin with the tip of his tongue. The velvety, moist caresses made her squirm again, and she threaded her fingers through his dark hair.

"Maddie." Her name was more a vibration, than a sound. "Do you understand now?"

Understand?

For an instant she wondered if Patrick had read her mind about understanding him.

"About...what?" Maddie managed to get out.

"About what I was saying."

It took another long minute to process the question, partly because she was so muddled. Patrick was still holding her, but he wasn't doing anything, and she really wanted him to keep doing what he'd been doing, which was kissing and touching her in all kinds of lovely places.

She remembered they'd discussed Ted being a louse. She wasn't entirely certain her ex-fiancé was a louse, just immature and thoughtless. They should have talked more over the years, but sometimes talking meant honesty, and neither one of them had really been willing to admit their teenage passion had fizzled like a wet firecracker. Even to themselves.

"Maddie?"

Jeez, why did Patrick have to start talking *now* of all times.

"What?" she said crossly.

"Do you believe me now, that you're attractive?"

Maddie's mouth tightened. So, he'd just been trying to demonstrate she wasn't such a dog when it came to being desirable, which meant nothing at all. She decided she was right after all. Men were...*men*. Maybe they couldn't help being rotten. She stiffened and tried to step backward, but she was trapped by the car, and Patrick's fingers still curved around her bottom.

Fine, she would just shove him away, that's what.

Her fingers were more reluctant than her mind to let go of such an attractive male, but she managed to free them from Patrick's hair.

"Sure, I believe you," she muttered, and pushed at his chest. He didn't budge, of course, it was like pushing at a rock face in El Morro. There wasn't any justice in the world.

She heard him sigh.

"What's wrong now?

"You," Maddie snapped. She tried to wiggle sideways and met with no more success than her previous efforts. "Let go of me."

"Not until we talk about it." Patrick wasn't about

to admit he was having trouble bringing his body under control, something he didn't want Maddie to see. Not that she couldn't have figured it out for herself, but she was so riled up—for reasons he couldn't begin to imagine—she obviously wasn't paying attention to the physical evidence.

Unless...there was another possibility he didn't want to think about. Maddie couldn't possibly be a virgin at the age of twenty-six. Her fiancé might have been a skunk, but he couldn't have been *that* slow off the mark.

Could he?

Patrick shook his head. He hadn't tried to seduce a virgin since he was a teenager. Not that he'd had a particular interest in virgins, but when you're a kid, the choices are limited. If Maddie was really *that* inexperienced, then she was even more vulnerable than he'd imagined.

God, Maddie lived with her feelings visible to everyone, making her doubly vulnerable to all the pitfalls and dangers in the world. He'd managed his emotions for so long it was unsettling to be around someone who felt both joy and sorrow with such abandon.

She wriggled, doing devastating things to his self-control. "I said to let me go."

Patrick raised one eyebrow. "I didn't just fall off the turnip truck. You're probably itching to slap my face, and this way you can't get much English into your swing, even if you do try."

"That's ridiculous."

"Not really. I bet you were too stunned to slap Ted, so you probably have a lot of pent-up anger to take out on someone. If I show up at dinner tonight with a bruise on my jaw, they'll all wonder who I've been fighting."

"Like I could ever bruise you," Maddie snapped. "I'd break my hand trying."

"You never know. So talk to me."

"All right," she said. "Let's talk about a guy who kisses a woman as some kind of stupid 'demonstration.' How would you feel if I'd kissed you to demonstrate something?"

"Guys aren't like women. We like kissing for any reason," Patrick said without thinking.

"That isn't...you aren't...you..." She let out an inarticulate shriek.

Jeez.

What was that cliché about the difference between men and women and their views on sex? *Men don't need a reason, they just need a place.* Right. To a certain extent it was true, but he could see Maddie's point. If he'd wanted to bolster her self-confidence, he should never have claimed he had a rational reason to kiss her. Especially when it was just an excuse— nothing about kissing Maddie was rational, he'd just wanted to make it sound that way after the fact.

"I guess we'll have to do it over again," Patrick said, his voice rumbling through the tightness in his chest. He didn't want to hurt Maddie; she'd been hurt enough.

"Do what?"

"Kiss. And I could try some other forms of persuasion."

Ignoring all the reasons he shouldn't take things further, Patrick slid his finger down Maddie's jaw, then her throat, settling on the first button of her dress. He hadn't been a wild teenage boy for nothing, and first thing he'd noticed about her dress that morning was that the buttons were *not* the decorative variety.

With the skill he'd developed by the time he was sixteen, he unfastened the first button one-handed. Beneath his fingers Maddie drew a sharp breath but remained silent. Three more buttons slid from their holes, and a satisfied smile curved Patrick's mouth when he eased his hand inside the opening. He liked front-clasp bras.

The pupils in her eyes dilated as the hooks were dispatched with equal dexterity.

"Anything to say?" he muttered.

"Like what?"

Like stop.

Patrick couldn't quite bring himself to suggest it—not when he didn't want to stop—so he lifted one shoulder. "I told you I wasn't the least bit nice, and this should prove it. What would your father say if he knew what I was doing?"

"He wouldn't say anything, he'd just shoot you. Daddy believes in the direct approach."

A grin pulled at Patrick's mouth. "And how would you feel about me getting shot?"

"That…he should have waited. At least for a minute." A peculiar mix of anticipation and dread filled Maddie's golden-brown eyes. She wanted to know what he thought of her body, and at the same time was afraid of finding out.

The chance that Maddie was a virgin was rapidly becoming a certainty in his mind, but he pushed the thought away. There were some things it was safer not to know.

Patrick leaned closer and pressed a kiss to her mouth as he eased his fingers around the feminine territory he'd uncovered. Freed of the silk bra, her breast plumped into his hand, her nipple hardening as he rubbed his palm across the sensitive tip. The sensation nearly drove him to his knees. It wasn't as if he'd never touched a woman before, but Maddie's scent and taste and essential innocence were an aphrodisiac.

No longer thinking of privacy or the fact he didn't have any business kissing Maddie, Patrick thrust his tongue deeper into her mouth. He'd always enjoyed kissing—long slow kissing that went on forever, and Maddie had a mouth he could spend a lifetime getting to know. Inexperienced or not, she had a natural talent for kissing that made a man appreciate being alive.

And her fingers…hell, he loved the feel of her curious fingers, touching him at the same time he explored the satin skin beneath her dress. He should have realized she'd be so sensual. Everything about Maddie was sensual, from the full curve of her lips to the pleasure she took in a bird crying as it soared across the sky.

He was on the verge of losing complete control when a bawdy shout and whistle from a passing motorboat brought him back to reality.

"Damn," he growled, taking a quick look over his shoulder. The boat was moving on, the occupant's interest already focused on something else. His body had blocked most of their view, so the person couldn't have seen anything more than a man kissing a woman. Thank heaven. At his worst he'd never been an exhibitionist, and despite Maddie's emotional candor, he didn't think she was, either.

He turned back and saw Maddie leaning against the Blazer, her dress in disarray. His body, still tight, turned up the pressure, trying to wrest control away from his mind and conscience. It probably wouldn't take much to seduce her, but he wasn't that kind of man.

"In case you didn't get the message," Patrick said deliberately, pressing his hips closer, "I happen to think you're very sexy. Incredibly sexy. And these..." He stroked a pert nipple. "Are the prettiest I've ever seen."

He meant it, too. Maddie's breasts were small, but they were round and up-tilted, with the loveliest shape. His father had always said more than a handful was just a waste, and Maddie was the sweetest of handfuls.

"Understand?" he asked roughly.

Maddie bobbed her head. The sensations cascading through her body were still so overwhelming she didn't know whether to be glad or upset he'd broken off the kiss. It had never been like that with Ted, both alarming and delicious and exciting at the same time.

Nothing had prepared her for Patrick O'Rourke. She wasn't certain she believed him about her breasts being that pretty, but the hard bulge pressed against her stomach was evidence he found *some*thing attractive about her.

Until she was a little less confused, it would have to be enough.

Chapter Six

"I can't get over how much you two look alike," declared Kathleen O'Rourke, staring from Beth to Maddie and back again.

Kathleen was the youngest of the O'Rourke siblings, and mother of darling three-year-old twin daughters. After dinner they'd started a game of Candyland with the girls, but Amy and Peggy had fallen asleep in the middle, their dark, curly heads on their mother's lap. It turned out that Patrick had four brothers, two older than him, and four younger sisters, but only Kathleen had any children.

"It shouldn't be so surprising, your girls are identical," Maddie said comfortably. She was used to her own extended family, so the ebb and flow of people in Pegeen O'Rourke's old house was dear and familiar.

What wasn't comfortable was seeing Patrick in the dining room. He was seated at the table, drinking coffee and debating football tactics with his brothers, and looking so darned gorgeous it made her wobbly all over again.

Had she really let him touch her like that?

It didn't seem possible, yet the imprint of his hard, knowing hands was still on her breasts, and she still felt a hot rush of blood whenever she thought about it. He hadn't said much afterward, just helped her back into the Blazer and returned to the radio station with a grim expression on his face. An hour later he'd stopped by the ad office, as impersonal as a stranger, and asked if she was ready to go. They'd barely talked on the ferry ride and long drive to his mother's place, and she didn't think he'd so much as glanced at her since arriving.

Maddie shifted restlessly, focusing on the cheerful game board lying on the floor. In a few years she might have been teaching her own children to play Candyland—if things had been different. She bit down on her bottom lip, wondering if she'd ever feel normal again.

"I recognize that look," Kathleen said in a low voice.

"What look?"

"That 'my world just fell apart' look. I've seen it often enough in the mirror." She sighed. "You see, my husband ran off with my best friend when I was pregnant with the girls."

Maddie's eyes opened wide. She felt horrid about finding Ted with another woman *before* the wedding, but she'd gotten off lightly considering what had happened to Kathleen. "That's awful. What happened to me...it wasn't..." Her voice trailed.

Kathleen shrugged. "Betrayal is betrayal."

"Have you ever considered getting married

again?'' Maddie blurted out, then bit her lip in consternation. She didn't know Kathleen well enough to ask that sort of question, and it certainly wasn't any of her business.

But Kathleen didn't seem offended. She stroked Amy's sleep-flushed face and shook her head. ''It might be different if it was just me, but I have to think about the girls,'' she said. ''I can't take the chance of them getting hurt.''

''That wouldn't happen with the right man,'' Beth said, clearly distressed for her sister-in-law. ''At least stay open to the possibility.''

Kathleen and Maddie shared an understanding look. Beth was expecting a baby, had a husband who adored her, and was probably the happiest woman alive. They may as well argue the earth wasn't round as try to convince her that the risks of falling in love might outweigh the benefits.

As if directed by an internal radar, Maddie's gaze was drawn again to Patrick. From her position on the floor, she mostly saw his profile. He seemed relaxed except for the hand splayed tautly on his thigh, out of sight beneath the dining room table.

He'd tensed earlier, almost imperceptibly, when Kane had suggested giving him a loan to expand KLMS. Of course Patrick had laughed it off with a joke about being independent, yet his underlying reaction puzzled Maddie. Independence was important, but it was as if there was a transparent wall between him and the rest of the O'Rourkes, one he didn't want anyone to get through.

Patrick turned his head and caught her watching him before she could look away. For once he was somber and unsmiling, and she squirmed uncomfortably. Was he thinking about how she'd looked with her dress unbuttoned, with his fingers teasing her nipples?

Maddie shivered.

Doubts were already creeping back. Nothing could change the fact he'd initially kissed her for reasons that had nothing to do with thinking she was attractive. He'd said as much. And just how much did it take a man to get aroused? She didn't know enough about men and sex to be sure of anything, much less about a man like Patrick.

All at once Patrick pushed back from the table and stood up. "Maddie, how about taking a walk with me?" he asked.

"Good idea," said Shannon. She was the eldest O'Rourke daughter, and so drop-dead glamorous that Maddie felt dowdy in comparison. "I need some exercise. I ate too much."

He looked pained. "Shannon, don't be ridiculous. You can't walk in those high heels."

His sister wrinkled her nose at him as she twirled her elegantly shod foot. "Always the charmer, aren't you, dear brother?"

"I can't help myself, I was born to be charming." Patrick looked back at Maddie. "How about it?"

"Uh, sure," she said, trying not to see the other O'Rourkes grin and nudge each other with their elbows. It must have seemed he was trying to get her alone, but Maddie didn't think so. Not for romantic reasons, anyway. It was obvious what happened that afternoon had been an accident he didn't want repeated.

Outside, the night air was crisp and frosty, though it was still early in the fall. The scent of wood smoke

mingled with the fragrance of evergreen and damp
earth. It seemed familiar, tickling something in the
back of her mind. She'd lived in Washington until
she was two years old, so it must be from the time in
her life she didn't consciously remember.

"Warm enough?" Patrick asked as they strode
down a dark, tree-lined path.

"I'm fine."

Before leaving he'd made sure she put on a jacket,
though he'd decided not to wear one himself. She'd
thought it was part of his macho male act, but maybe
not. She wasn't used to the damp air in the Northwest;
he might be.

"I wanted to talk to you," he murmured after several minutes of silence.

"Could have fooled me."

"What's that supposed— Never mind." Patrick
stopped and stuck his fingers in his pockets. "I keep
thinking about this afternoon."

"Me, too. It seems strange to visit your family so
soon after we…uh, did *that*."

"We didn't do anything, that's the point," he said
sharply. "It just happened."

Maddie rolled her eyes. Maybe things like that
"just happened" to Patrick, but it seemed more dramatic to her. It wasn't every day a girl found out what
she'd been missing when it came to kissing and other
extracurricular activities.

"It seemed like something to me," she muttered.

"Right, and that's what I've been worried about."

"Oh."

"The thing is, I shouldn't have kissed you in the
first place. It wasn't right after everything you'd been
through."

"I would have objected if I didn't like it."

Patrick smiled wryly. Yeah, Maddie would have objected. She had a mind of her own and said whatever she thought.

"I want to be honest with you, because your ex-fiancé obviously wasn't," he said. "I think you're terrific, but I'm not a marrying kind of man. Even if I was, I couldn't think about it until I was sure the station was a success. I've been afraid you might have gotten the wrong idea."

The wrong idea? What was it with Patrick and "ideas."

She straightened. "You *what?*"

Warning tension sneaked up his spine. "You're so innocent, I thought you might have read more into us kissing…like that. It should never have gone that far. Not that it went anywhere, just not where it should have." He shook his head, knowing he sounded like an idiot. Maddie did that to him, driving sane thought from his brain and replacing it with drivel. "I take full responsibility."

"Isn't that nice of you."

"Maddie—"

"No." Maddie poked her finger in Patrick's chest. She didn't know whether to laugh or be furious. "I am not a child and I don't need you trying to protect me or apologize for something I could have stopped on my own."

"I'm older and should have known better."

"So being 'older' makes you think I want to marry you because of one little kiss?" She deliberately made her voice incredulous.

"It wasn't so little."

"It was a kiss, that's all. Isn't that what you've been saying? How dumb do you think I am?"

He winced. "I don't think you're dumb."

"Could have fooled me. We barely know each other, I just got cheated on by my fiancé, and you keep thinking I'm going to get ideas about us spending the rest of our lives together. At the moment I'm not even sure I like you, why would I want a lifetime?"

"I guess I deserve that."

"I'm trying to figure out what to do with my life," Maddie continued irately. "I'm certainly not thinking about marrying anyone. I thought I made that clear. *You* certainly have, so I don't know why we're having this discussion again."

"Yeah, right."

Her reaction was stinging Patrick's pride, but he was smart enough to keep his mouth shut on the subject. It *had* been an arrogant assumption, but Maddie was different from other women—innocent and idealistic, despite what happened with her fiancé. She was exactly the type to start seeing him through rose-colored glasses. If only she could understand that he kept doing and saying the wrong thing because he was afraid of hurting her. And now he had a sneaking suspicion that he'd wounded her in some other way.

"Beth and Kane offered to take me back to the bed-and-breakfast place. I'd better see if they're ready to leave," Maddie said.

There was a stiff dignity in her voice that didn't suit the Maddie he knew, but Patrick just nodded. He didn't know what would happen if Kane found out about the way he'd kissed Maddie. His brother adored his new wife, and if Maddie was Beth's sister, then Kane would be protective of her, as well.

For a guy who liked to keep things simple, his life was going to hell in a hurry.

His best bet was to keep out of Maddie's way. It would be hard with her working at the radio station, but that's the way it had to be.

Maddie typed a few words into her computer, then put her chin on her hand and stared at the screen without really seeing the display. In the past two weeks Patrick had barely spoken to her. He'd treated her exactly the way she'd first wanted, like any other employee. Kane and Beth had taken her home, and while she'd spent time with the O'Rourkes since then, Patrick had been conspicuously absent.

Her mother always said to be careful what you asked for, and this might be one of those occasions. How could she begin to figure him out when he barely said good morning to her?

I think you're terrific, but I'm not a marrying kind of man.

Thinking about Patrick's absurd "warning" still annoyed Maddie. How many times did he think she had to be warned? He'd said he wasn't "nice," he'd said he didn't want to get married or have children. As a matter of fact, he'd said a whole lot of things that were perfectly irritating.

"Darn him," she said beneath her breath.

Heaven knew she had plenty of things to think about besides Patrick, like the fact she had a new sister and brother-in-law, when she'd lived her whole life as an only child. Though the O'Rourkes had treated her connection to Beth as a foregone conclusion, they'd gone ahead and done the research to confirm it. Kane had even paid for some expensive genetic tests, the results coming back the same day his investigators got their hands on the adoption records for both Beth and herself.

So now she had a twin sister. An identical twin.

Her parents planned to fly out soon to meet Beth and had talked to her by phone several times. Once they'd gotten over their dismay over the girls being separated, they'd been thrilled that Maddie had found a sister. Some adoptive parents might have been threatened when their kid went looking for a birth family, but not her mom and dad. They were the greatest.

Sighing quietly, Maddie corrected a typo in one of the graphics. She needed to concentrate on the new advertising campaign. Stephen seemed to like her ideas, so at least she was doing all right in the employment department.

Just not in the heart department.

Maddie gave up and gazed out the window. It was a stormy day and everyone had been complaining about it raining for the past several days. They'd also been coming down with stomach flu in record numbers, leaving the station short staffed.

"Is the weather getting to you?" Stephen asked, breaking her reverie. "You don't get this much rain in New Mexico."

She pasted a smile on her lips and shook her head. "No. I like it, it's what keeps everything green."

"That's what Patrick always says."

Patrick.

Great. Couldn't she go one minute without thinking about the man? He was driving her crazy with his polite nods when they passed in the hallway or met in the break room. It wasn't that she wanted him to kiss her again, but why had he suddenly started treating her like a contagious disease?

"You're doing an excellent job. I told him you were responsible for those new advertisers. He was pleased."

Oh, goody.

"I'm going to take a break and get a cup of coffee," she said, unable to contain her restlessness. "Can I bring you anything?"

"No, I still have some of Candy's French roast in my thermos."

This time Maddie's smile was genuine. There had been a few raised eyebrows when the Formidable Finn started making the advertising director a thermos of coffee every morning, but her stern demeanor kept everyone silent. It had been a simple matter to suggest Candy make an extra thermos for Stephen, with the excuse it was just going to waste at home. And it shouldn't take more than a few nudges to get them together, especially since she'd learned Stephen was the source of Candy's whimsical cat jewelry—all from years of Christmas gift exchanges and "gestures of appreciation."

Going into the break room she saw Candy making a cup of tea. "How are you? Any sign of the dreaded flu?"

"So far so good. I don't get sick easily. Is Stephen all right?" she asked anxiously.

"He's fine," Maddie assured her new friend. "Did you know he calls you Candy now in private? And he won't touch a drop of anyone else's coffee."

Candy turned pink. She'd stopped pulling her hair

back from her face so harshly, and looked quite lovely as a result. There hadn't been any sign of Stephen asking her out on a date, but Maddie was convinced her handsome supervisor was more than interested.

"I wish you could have shown up twenty years ago," Candy said wistfully.

"Twenty years ago I wouldn't have been much help. I was more interested in playing with dolls than anything else."

"Then I—" Candy fell silent as Patrick appeared at the door. "I'd better get back to my desk." She walked past Patrick, giving Maddie a wink he couldn't see.

"Something going on?" he asked.

"Not a thing." Maddie hurriedly poured herself a cup of coffee from the office pot. She turned, wondering if Patrick would have that same darned polite expression he'd been wearing the past two weeks.

It was so frustrating.

He'd touched her in ways no man had ever touched her, but now he acted as if they were practically strangers.

Which they were, Maddie acknowledged silently. And he'd made it plain things weren't going to change, either.

Drat it all. She didn't have any experience with men beyond her relationship with Ted, and he'd hardly been any help in understanding how things were between men and women.

A wry humor made her shake her head. *Ted.* They'd been children playing at being adults, never going past the stage of holding hands and following the rules of "No hands above the waist in the front, and none below the waist." Healthy rules meant to protect them both, enforced with a father's glare and a warning that few boys would ignore.

Maddie sipped her coffee and looked at Patrick from under her lashes. He definitely wasn't a boy. And she doubted there was a single rule he hadn't broken.

There hadn't been many "bad" boys in Slapshot, but she recognized the faint remnants of Patrick's days as a teenage tough. Maybe it was the hint of a sexy swagger when he walked, or the midafternoon beard shadow that gave him an aura of dark danger. Or a dozen other things that made him so very... interesting.

Maddie, Maddie. Haven't you learned anything? chided a voice in her head. If she couldn't trust the boy she'd grown up with, how could she trust a man like Patrick O'Rourke?

She couldn't, that's what.

"Stephen says you're doing a fantastic job," he commented, pouring the last of the coffee into a cup and unplugging the pot. "I understand you're working on a proposal for new billboards to advertise the station. I'll look forward to seeing it."

"Uh-huh."

"Yes, well, I'd better get back to my office."

She made a face at his retreating back. It wasn't that she didn't appreciate Patrick giving her a job, she just wished he wasn't being so standoffish. *He* was the one who'd decided to kiss her, not the other way around.

Okay, maybe she did want him to kiss her again. Sort of like an experiment, to see if she would still react the same way.

And if *he'd* react.

Maddie blushed furiously at the notion of Patrick getting aroused because of her. She was pretty sure he'd felt that way, but her experience was limited, and doubt was insidious. She'd heard it was easy for women to pretend a response, but could men fake it? Had she been right thinking he'd responded in the first place? Patrick had been pressed against her and he was quite…impressive down there. She could have been misunderstood.

"Boy, are you mixed up," Maddie told herself.

The station seemed practically deserted with so many people out sick. She'd just stopped to smile at the DJ—best known as the Seattle Kid—when he began frantically waving at her. She tiptoed inside.

The DJ thrust the headset and microphone at her. "Gotta go. The music's almost done," he groaned, making a mad dash out the door, one hand clapped over his mouth.

Maddie stared at the headset a full ten seconds.

To her relief the technician walked in at that moment, but he backed away with a horrified expression, shaking his head when she tried to hand him the microphone. He began making motions with his hands, obviously urging action, but she didn't know anything about the equipment in the booth.

"They're expecting DJ chatter. Say something," Jeremy said in a loud stage whisper. "You're live."

He pointed to the On Air sign lighted up on the wall, and Maddie started feeling a little nauseous herself. The motto of KLMS was Nothing Is Worse Than Dead Air, but she wasn't sure it applied to a novice with just two weeks' experience in the ad department.

"Uh…hello," she said into the mike, to Jeremy's obvious relief, who continued to make encouraging motions. "This is Maddie Jackson, and I'm…uh, filling in for the Seattle Kid, who seems to have suddenly come down with the stomach flu like most everyone else who works here."

She cleared her throat, put her coffee down and sat in the recently vacated chair. The electronic board in front of her looked like something out of *Star Trek* with its blinking lights and dials. There was no way she could figure out how to play something without help.

"And for those of you uttering a sympathetic murmur of support, I'm sure he appreciates it. I have to confess this whole radio thing is new to me. I'm from a little town in New Mexico called Slapshot and haven't been in the Seattle area for very long. We'll figure out how to play some music for you in a minute, but in the meantime…" She paused, desperately trying to remember what sort of things DJs talked about on the radio.

Jeremy kept up his hand signals and Maddie took so many fast breaths she was in danger of hyperventilating. She was petrified. There were literally thousands of people listening to her, and for once in her life she couldn't think of anything to say.

"I'd like to talk about…kissing. And men," she blurted out, only to see Jeremy abandon his signaling and clamp his hands over his head.

Okay, maybe kissing wasn't the best subject. But at least there wasn't any dead air to worry about.

Chapter Seven

Patrick stared at the container of aspirin on his desk. Since Maddie had come to work at KLMS he'd practically emptied the economy-size bottle; pretty soon it would eat an economy-size hole in his tummy. Maddie was making him crazy—even crazier than having sixty percent of his employees out sick because they'd gotten a twenty-four-hour virus that was turning into a week-long siege in the bathroom.

Kissing her had been a huge mistake, no matter how good it felt at the time. He could see the confusion in her face every time she looked at him now. And why shouldn't she? She came from a world where intimate kisses meant something.

It did *mean something,* said the internal voice that reminded him of his father.

The voice was constantly with him these days, no matter how hard he tried not to hear it. If he *had* acknowledged the voice, he would have reminded it that he'd only just met Maddie, they were little more than strangers, so how much could a kiss between them mean?

The memory of Maddie's kiss-swollen lips, dazed eyes and the tantalizing rise and fall of her breasts filled his head, and he groaned.

More than anything he was furious with himself. How could he have kissed Maddie in the first place? It was bad enough that he'd lost control with a complete innocent, but Maddie was recovering from a broken heart. It smacked of taking advantage, and the O'Rourkes had a code about women that was as old as Ireland. Never, in all the outrageous things he'd done as a kid, had he done something he thought would hurt a girl.

Then he'd gone and stuffed his foot in his mouth, trying to tell Maddie not to get any ideas about marriage. That had been arrogant of him. No wonder she was so offended.

"Boy, do I have a problem," he muttered, tossing down a couple more aspirin tablets.

The radio was playing on his desk, set to a low volume, and for some reason it sounded like Maddie—probably because he couldn't stop thinking about her. With a sigh he turned up the dial to hear what was going on in the broadcast booth.

"...he's a little old-fashioned, but that isn't the problem. I mean, my dad is old-fashioned, and he's wonderful," said the voice.

It *was* Maddie.

Patrick shook his head to clear it, unable to believe what he was hearing. How could a scatterbrain like Maddie get herself on his radio station?

"And he's a great kisser, but now he acts like I'm kryptonite or something. I could swear he was interested…you know, physically, but maybe I was wrong. Can a man fake that kind of thing?''

Oh…*no*.

Patrick lunged from his chair, only to fall flat on his face when his feet tangled with the trash can.

''Does anyone out there know why men are so confusing?'' Maddie continued. ''Maybe a man could explain it, though we probably confuse you, too. It must be all that 'men are from Mars' stuff I've heard about. I have to admit we *do* seem to be from different planets. And I told you how he feels about marriage. To tell the truth, I'm not sure why he's so much against it, but you'd think it was worse than being boiled in oil.''

Muttering curses, Patrick limped as quickly as possible to the broadcast booth. Maddie was perched on the corner of the console, still chattering away about marriage and kissing and men, and asking one and all for their opinion. Jeremy Hollings seemed to be in shock, but when he saw Patrick's face, he dissolved into laughter.

Patrick made a slashing motion across his throat, but Maddie just returned with a helpless gesture and pointed to the microphone as if it explained everything.

He pushed inside the booth.

''Announce a song,'' he snarled.

''I don't know how to play one,'' she said, then sighed. ''Oops, everyone, I was talking to the owner. Mr. O'Rourke wants me to play something, which I guess is the point since this *is* a country music station. We'll get some Garth Brooks going as soon as I figure out how to work these dials. Honestly, the equipment in here is so complicated you'd think it was designed for the space program.''

Patrick snatched a CD from the rack, stuffed it into the right slot and started the music. Just to be safe he disconnected Maddie's microphone and headset, then scowled.

''What in hell are you doing?''

''Mack got sick and you said there's nothing worse than dead air on the radio. So I just talked.''

''You…'' Patrick kicked the door shut so Jeremy wouldn't be able to hear them. ''That isn't what I meant.''

The hurt expression he dreaded filled her eyes.

''But I talked about how great the Crockett Café is, and told everyone that the Liberty Market is now open twenty-four hours a day. They're two of KLMS advertisers. I didn't break any of the FCC rules. I'm sure I didn't, so what's the big deal?''

''You were talking about me! That's the big deal.''

''Not by name. How could anyone know it was you?''

She didn't get it.

She just didn't have a clue.

Anybody who knew them would put two and two together and come up with 250.

''You shouldn't have said anything about me, period.''

''Why not? You *are* a good kisser.''

''How would you know? You don't have anything worth comparing it against. You wouldn't know a good kiss from a bad one.''

''Are you saying you *aren't* a good kisser?''

''Yes. *No!* That isn't what I…'' He ground his teeth together. Maddie was doing it to him again, and he had only himself to blame. "All right. I'll figure out a way to clean up this mess later. In the meantime, let's get out of here. We have to talk."

"But Mack is too sick to finish, and there's nobody to handle his show."

Patrick looked at the clock on the wall and realized it would be at least an hour before his next DJ and her producer arrived. *If* they arrived and hadn't been caught by the flu along with everyone else.

The week was just getting better all the time.

"Go back to your desk. I'll take care of the booth until Lindsay Markoff arrives." He crossed his fingers, hoping that Lindsay would arrive early. Maybe he could call and make sure she was coming. She was always wanting more airtime, anyway, and he'd make it up in her paycheck.

Maddie seemed doubtful. "I thought you hated talking on the radio."

"I'm not going to talk," Patrick snarled. He knew he wasn't being fair. Maddie had done her best to help out, and now he was taking out his frustration on her. He tried to calm down. "I'll just play the music and ad tapes until someone else gets here."

"But they're usually announced," Maddie argued. "The songs and all."

"At the beginning of the sets, yes, but..." Defeated, Patrick pushed her down in the chair. "All right, I'll work the console, you announce the upcoming song sets. *Just* the sets," he added hastily. Giving Maddie a forum for her runaway tongue was the last thing he wanted.

Just then Jeremy stuck his head inside the booth and Patrick glared. "Why didn't you stop her?" he demanded. "Why didn't you start the music or run an ad or something?"

"Hey, boss, I'm just a lowly little technician. Mack gave Maddie the headphones and you know how I freeze on the air. I just wanted you to know the phone bank is lighting up—folks want to give Maddie some advice about that great kisser she knows." He grinned.

Patrick gave him a stern look, but Jeremy was irrepressible. He probably thought Maddie talking her head off was a grand joke. A twenty-year-old former juvenile delinquent and electronic genius, Jeremy was working at the station while getting his degree in communication. He'd probably end up as the next Ted Turner, but in the meantime he was a pain in the butt. Of course, having been a juvenile delinquent once himself, Patrick understood the kid.

"No phones," he ordered.

"But, boss, we *like* phone calls at KLMS," Jeremy said with a perfectly straight face. "You always say—"

"Never mind what I always say," Patrick said. "Get back out there and tell the callers that you're sorry, but Maddie doesn't know how to work the phones any better than she knows how to play music."

Jeremy walked out, shaking his head in a sorrowful display of disappointment. His lanky body settled in the producer's chair, a position he'd been coveting for the simple reason it gave him power. Patrick sent him a warning glance as he eyed the blinking phone bank. Jeremy might be destined for greatness, but he was dead meat if he tried to send one of those calls through to the booth.

"All right," Patrick growled to Maddie. "I'll put on some commercials, then after that you announce we're doing a long music set, starting out with Lee Greenwood's, 'God Bless the U.S.A.'"

"Oh, I like that song."

"No editorials," Patrick said instantly. If Maddie strayed from the script, she would *really* stray. God knew he was taking a chance letting her remain in the broadcast booth, but either he got on the radio himself—something he'd sworn never to do—or he took a chance.

She wouldn't break any of those FCC rules that everyone else worried about, she'd just spill her life story, along with his and everyone else's she knew. He'd keep his hand on the switch to cut her off, just in case.

Her look called into question his intelligence, but he didn't relent. There were some things a man had to do to stay sane. He reminded himself that her sweet, artless revelations were a far cry from the polished DJ patter radio audiences had come to expect. So his decision was the best for the station and didn't have much to do with him.

Really.

Honestly, Maddie couldn't understand why Patrick was so upset. He drove the Blazer away from the station with a grim twist to his mouth that hadn't changed since he'd charged into the broadcast booth.

The DJ for the next show had arrived early, so they'd only needed to do the Seattle Kid's show for another seventeen minutes. But she didn't know what Patrick was planning to do. Now that they were alone, he was being awfully quiet.

Maybe he was going to fire her and wanted to tell her away from the station so she wouldn't make a fuss in front of everyone. The thought made Maddie slump down in the passenger seat, thoroughly depressed.

It was hard enough being so confused about men, but now she might get fired?

"Aren't you going to say something?" she asked.

Patrick swung into the busy parking lot of a chain restaurant out by the highway, then sat for a long minute with his hands on the steering wheel.

"I'm sorry, but I thought I was helping," Maddie added rebelliously.

She *had* been doing a good job for the station. It was one thing to get fired because she couldn't do the work, but going on the radio hadn't been her fault, it was because everyone was sick and she'd been in the right place at the wrong time. Patrick was being completely unreasonable.

He sighed. "I know. You were doing exactly what anyone else would have done, and I apologize for overreacting."

Maddie crossed her arms over her stomach and stared out the window. Rain was streaming over the windshield, and their breath was clouding the glass. The damp cold was alien to her, and for the first time since coming to Washington she felt a twinge of homesickness that had nothing to do with missing her parents.

New Mexico was a dry land, painted by red rock and the gold of grass that died swiftly in the parched heat of summer. She missed the *ristras* that decorated the houses with their brilliant dried peppers, and the limitless sky rising over the Magdalenas. The smell of sage and piñon pine had been replaced by the scent of evergreen, and even if it struck a chord deep inside her, this place wasn't home.

"I don't belong here," she whispered.

"God, Maddie, don't say that. I feel awful enough for yelling at you." Patrick rubbed his hand over his face, shaking his head at the same time. "You belong."

"All right, I don't belong *to* anyone here."

"You have Beth and Kane and the rest of us."

"You keep warning me that I *don't* have you, Patrick. It can't be both ways."

She sensed, rather than saw him reach out in the gray light inside the cab. He lifted her hand and squeezed it, then laced their fingers together.

"I'm lousy with this kind of thing," he admitted after a moment. "I don't want to hurt or disappoint anyone. I just want to keep things nice and simple. I messed up bad as a kid, Maddie. Something happened to me when my father died. I don't ever want to feel that way again. It's better to keep things uncomplicated."

"That's convenient."

He released her hand and drew back. "What's that supposed to mean?"

"Nothing. Everything."

Maddie shivered and gathered her jacket closer around her throat. With a low apology Patrick turned the engine back on and notched the heat up. For a minute the air blowing from the vents was cold, then welcome warmth spread across her feet.

"What do you mean?" he asked again.

"It seems to me you keep everyone at arm's length. Even your family."

"Don't be ridiculous. I might be spending a lot of time at the station lately, but normally I eat dinner with the family a couple times a month."

"There's a difference between being *with* them and just being there."

He snorted.

Maddie stuck her feet more fully under the flow of warmth from the vent and tried to find a way to explain. Maybe she was wrong, but she'd seen Patrick with the O'Rourkes and it bothered her. In some ways he was so alone. She couldn't imagine him talking to his mother the way she'd been pouring her heart out every night with her parents. She might have run away from Slapshot, but she hadn't run away from them.

"You smile and joke around," she said. "You kiss your mother and play with your nieces, but there's a barrier between you and the rest of the world. It's as if you don't want anyone to get too close, so you keep them away with your smiles and laid-back attitude."

"You're full of it."

"Pegeen is worried," Maddie added softly. "She thinks Kane getting married has something to do with you not coming around so much."

Patrick's jaw was rigid as he shook his head. "That's a bunch of nonsense. I took a risk when I switched KLMS to country music, and then Kane's romance with Beth helped put the station on the map. I've been busy, that's all. There's no mystery or deep psychological stuff going on, it's plain-and-simple economics."

"But—"

"No." He seemed ready to explode, a far cry from the smiling, nonchalant guy she'd first met. "Not

wanting things to be complicated means just that, *not complicated.''*

Maddie blinked, trying not to cry. Patrick had a wonderful family, but he didn't want to get too close, or admit he cared that much, because something might happen. The way something had happened to his father. She hadn't needed Kane's explanation that the death of Keenan O'Rourke had come at a terrible time for Patrick—a time when he was too young to be a child and not old enough to be a man.

She didn't want to be like that, did she?

Alone?

It was something to think about. Because no matter how much it could hurt to love someone, the alternative might be worse.

"Jeez," Patrick muttered. "I apologize, and then blow up again. It's just that I feel so guilty."

It was the last thing Maddie expected to hear. "About what? If you're going to apologize for being in a bad mood you'd better apologize to everyone at the station. Stephen says he's never seen you so surly."

"He's seen me plenty surly."

"Since when?"

"Since I was a dumb kid doing my best to get arrested or killed. *All right?*"

Her breath seemed frozen in her lungs. She didn't know Patrick that well, but the dark glitter of his eyes and intensity of his voice was…surprising. Or maybe it wasn't, because she'd known all along that Patrick wasn't quite as comfortable as he wanted the world to think.

"I said I was a teenage tough, but you can't imagine what that really means, can you?" he asked furiously. "I drank, smoked, slept with every skirt I could catch and fought dirty. I even tried to steal a truck. It's a miracle I didn't end up in prison or juvie, and even more of a miracle that my family didn't have to see me lying on a table in the morgue. What a treat *that* would have been after burying my father."

"You were angry because you missed him."

"Damned straight. So I became the toughest, meanest kid you ever met. I'll demonstrate." He reached out and deliberately, crudely, put his hand over her breast. "I'm not the kind of guy who would have waited for a wedding band to get you under me. And I wouldn't have cared if it happened in a bed. A car seat would have been just fine."

She wanted to be furious, to slap his hand away, but a rebellious heat spread out from the fingers moving over her nipple, shimmering into the deepest recesses of her abdomen. And some instinct she hadn't known she possessed told her that Patrick was hurting himself far worse than he could hurt her.

"Do you hear me?" he demanded in the silence.

"I hear you."

"Good. Then you understand."

Instead of shrinking farther away, Maddie unsnapped her seat belt and leaned into his hand. Her tummy was turning to shivering jelly, especially when his touch gentled, his thumb brushing over the sensitive peak.

His heavy-lidded gaze dropped to her breasts. He couldn't help but see and feel the responsive hardness of her nipples. The shivering turned into an internal earthquake.

She still wasn't confident of her feminine appeal, but she did know there was more to life than watching it go by. And she knew Patrick had elected to sit on the sidelines. He kept trying to scare her away and she didn't know why. It wasn't a secret how he felt about marriage and children; he'd made it abundantly clear he planned to spend his life as a bachelor. If anything happened between them, it wouldn't be without her knowing the score.

"Actually, I *don't* understand," Maddie whispered.

"Then I should explain it better." With a muttered curse he pulled her across the transmission. He tugged her astride his hips, and for the second time in her life his arousal was pressed hard and intimately against Maddie. Only this time it touched a place that turned to fire at the contact. A low moan escaped, and her fingers dug into his shoulders.

"Oh, for pity's sake, *why aren't you stopping me?*" Patrick bellowed. "After what happened with your wedding you're supposed to hate men."

"Just men who cheat. My problem is not being able to tell the difference."

He was trying to shock her enough to say "No," but it wasn't going to work since she knew saying "no" would end the conversation. And she was perfectly safe because Patrick was too scrupulous about the O'Rourke "code" to force a woman. She'd heard all about that code from Beth.

Maddie squirmed on Patrick's lap, adjusting her legs into a less-strained position, only to hear him groan.

"Is something wrong?" she asked.

"Nobody's that innocent," he growled.

"So, can you fake that?" she asked brightly. There wasn't any question of what "that" was, not with it snuggled into her feminine heat, separated by only a few layers of clothing.

Patrick hit his head against the window in frustration. He had his hands full of a sexy lady who was rapidly turning the tables on him. Maddie was understandably curious about sex and men and her inhibitions were dissolving at the speed of light. What she lacked in experience she made up for in sheer instinctive guile. It ought to make him furious, but instead he wanted to kiss her.

"No, I can't fake it." He wished to heaven he *had* been faking his arousal, because it wouldn't hurt so much. "And I can't believe you asked that on the radio. We're a country music station, not true confessions."

"I didn't come right out and say it."

Patrick swallowed the chuckle rising in his chest. "Close enough. You're a hazard, you know that? Someone ought to declare you off-limits."

"I thought you already did."

"To who?"

"To you, of course. Two weeks and you've barely said good morning to me."

She'd melted bonelessly over him, the way only a woman could manage, and he was having trouble keeping his hands away from the obvious battlegrounds of sexual conquest. Actually, he found all parts of a woman's body sexy, from the arches of the foot to the sensitive place behind her ears. He finally settled for Maddie's waist. It seemed like a compromise, but it also reminded him of the sweet curves above, and the tempting warmth below.

"I've said more than good morning," he said.

"Yeah, you added 'good night' a couple days ago. What a shock."

His laugh was both a release and exquisite torture as she rocked with him. He sighed. "What am I going to do about you, Maddie?"

"I don't recall asking you to do anything."

"Mmm, yes."

The mental picture he carried of Maddie as a ditzy airhead was fading into something more complex, more worrisome and infinitely tempting.

They were on opposite poles, a woman who felt too much and a man who didn't want to feel at all.

What was happening to him? He was the unflappable one in the family, the kidder, the comfortable brother who didn't get stirred up along with everyone else. He just sat back and let everything flow by. And he liked it that way.

So why should his peace of mind be threatened by a "nice" girl from a town he'd never heard of before?

Good question, son.

Oh, be quiet, he ordered crossly.

If his father *was* talking to him, then he was way off base when it came to Maddie. She was a luscious bundle, but she'd never be *his* luscious bundle.

Let his brothers and sisters get married and give his mother grandchildren.

Grandchildren?

Patrick broke out into a sweat, realizing he'd subconsciously associated Maddie and children together. It was probably because they'd talked several times about babies, though he couldn't be certain.

He closed his eyes, but he couldn't shut out Maddie's warmth, covering him like a blanket. Hell, he'd cultivated a comfortable laid-back attitude toward women over the years. A "treat them nice, but take them or leave them" sort of perspective.

Now he didn't know what to think.

Maddie unsettled him in a way he hadn't felt in a long while, and it didn't feel nearly as terrible as he'd thought it would.

Chapter Eight

When they got back to the station Maddie gave him a faint smile, then disappeared down the corridor to the ad office.

Oh, man. He hadn't even kissed her, and she smiled like the first Eve, reminding Adam of the fundamental differences between man and woman.

"Patrick, we have to talk," declared Dixie Saunders, grabbing his arm before he could get farther than the reception area.

"What is it, Dix?"

"It's about Maddie's new show."

Damn.

"Don't worry, it was a mistake, Dix. Maddie doesn't have a new show, she was just filling in when Mack had to run for the rest room. He's the latest victim of the flu."

"But it was a wonderful mistake," Dixie exclaimed. "The phones haven't stopped ringing. The men are calling just as much as the women, so there's cross-gender appeal. You know how hard that is to get. Everyone wants to know who the mysterious kisser is and offer Maddie advice.''

The knowing look in Dixie's eyes made Patrick grit his teeth. He'd never fully appreciated how private he was, and having Maddie talk about him like that, albeit anonymously, was galling.

''Forget it, Dix.'' He headed for his own office with Dixie tagging along at his heels.

''But you could have a huge hit on your hands. Let Maddie do a segment on advice for the lovelorn. People could call in and explain their problem, then others could give their opinion, say what worked for them, and she could just...''

''What? Be herself?'' Patrick finished, his tone ironic.

He opened the door of his office and Dixie scooted in ahead of him.

''You have to admit she's a sweetheart.''

He gave Dixie a repressive look. Not that he expected it to do any good. She was a great producer and extremely ambitious. And she might even be right about Maddie becoming a success on the radio; he just didn't want it to be on *his* radio station.

Thankfully his phone rang and he pointed toward the door. ''I appreciate the input. We'll talk about it another time.''

Dixie left reluctantly, and Patrick had to smile at her reproachful expression. It wasn't every day a radio station was flooded with phone calls about one of their programs, and he was probably missing a great opportunity. But his nerves couldn't handle the idea of Maddie broadcasting to the greater Puget Sound area.

He lifted the receiver on the fourth ring of the phone. "KLMS Radio. O'Rourke, here."

"Hey, I caught your new approach to talk radio," said Kane. "I'm not into that sort of thing, but the show was really interesting. Quite illuminating, if you know what I mean."

For a moment Patrick froze. He hadn't thought about his *family* hearing Maddie. They would think he'd been putting the moves on her, when he really hadn't. At least, not in the way it must have sounded.

"Kane."

"Yup. Beth and I were working down at the Crockett Crisis Center, listening to the radio to pass the time. Then Maddie's program came on. I must say it generated a fair amount of interest."

"It wasn't a program, it was an emergency. Mack got so sick that someone had to drive him home, and Maddie ended up with the headphones and mike."

"Nice of her to help out."

Kane's chuckle sounded faintly evil—a sound Patrick recognized. It was the same chuckle Patrick had used when Kane and Beth were courting. Not that Patrick was courting Maddie or anyone else, but it was payback time for his brother.

"Don't you have better things to do than harass a hardworking radio station manager?" he asked. "You should be making love to your wife, not bothering me."

"Any reason I can't do both?"

"Stop teasing him," said Beth in the background. Her soft laugh was followed by the rumble of Kane's voice, low and intimate, the way it always was when he talked to his wife.

Patrick sank back in his chair, shocked by the swift

envy he felt. He'd never envied his brother, though once upon a time he'd resented the way Kane had tried to take the place of their father. But it was pure, unadulterated envy filling him now, envy of the way his brother and sister-in-law lived in their own special world, loving each other beyond reason.

No.

His head shook in instant denial. What Kane and Beth shared might be nice, but it wasn't for him. He wasn't interested in the usual things, like love and marriage and children. He'd never let emotional chaos into his life again, which is exactly what would happen if he fell in love. Maddie was a dangerous influence, thinking with her heart rather than her head, running headlong toward pain and hurt and pulling him along with her. By nature the O'Rourkes were too passionate and driven by their emotions; he couldn't let that part of him take control, ever again.

"Look," Patrick said finally. "I wouldn't hurt Maddie, you know that. Something happened between us that shouldn't have, but I'm handling it."

"I know." Kane sounded surprised, as if he hadn't needed the reassurance. "Are you coming to dinner on Sunday? Maddie is teaching Mom and Beth how to make homemade tamales and green chili stew."

Patrick hesitated. He hadn't planned on going, but staying away would convince Maddie even more that he had a problem when it came to being with the family.

"Sure, I'll be there."

With a fire extinguisher, he added silently, remembering the Tabasco sauce Maddie had shaken over her French fries. He made a mental note to bring a couple of pizzas and a carton of chicken with him, just in case.

Spicy was one thing, suicide by fire was another.

"Canned peppers don't really taste the same as New Mexico chilies," Maddie said, frowning into space as she sampled the green chili stew. "They don't have any heat."

Patrick made a choking sound behind her, but she ignored him, the same way she'd ignored his teasing about everyone needing an asbestos mouth to eat her cooking. She'd noticed him sneaking more than one bite of the fresh salsa she'd made to go with the nachos, so he obviously liked spicy food better than he claimed.

Ostensibly the O'Rourkes were all in the kitchen "helping" with dinner, but it didn't take twelve people to cook a meal. They were mostly joking around, chatting and catching up on the week's news. A favorite topic was Beth and Kane's baby, and though it still gave Maddie a twinge to think about babies, she enjoyed the give and take of the family.

Her own family was the same—big and boisterous, full of laughter and nosy about everyone else's business. Boy, were the Jacksons nosy. Everyone kept calling, asking how things were going, and generally trying to be supportive. They were driving her crazy, but it was really very sweet. Her uncle had even offered to help tar and feather Ted if it would make her feel better, but she'd assured him it wasn't necessary.

"We should have gotten some beer to go with all this spicy stuff," said Patrick.

Pegeen fixed him with her sharp eyes. "Not in my house, young man."

Beth and Pegeen had caught on quickly to the art of making tamales. They'd declared Shannon a disaster in the kitchen and relegated her to setting the dining room table, while Patrick and his four brothers were assigned salad duty. Kathleen was working on dessert, a chocolaty Mexican concoction that Maddie particularly loved.

"A master's degree in business, an executive of Kane Enterprises, and here I am, chopping tomatoes," grumped Neil O'Rourke.

"Better than onions," complained Kane good-naturedly. His attractive nose wrinkled at the pungent scent rising from the cutting board.

"Hey, I'm the only one who's really working here," Patrick said. He sat in the corner, lazily shaking the cruet of tart salad dressing Maddie had assembled more than twenty minutes before. Tiger Lily, Pegeen's butterscotch tabby cat, was perched smugly across his legs. She seemed to know she'd found the most indolent lap in the house.

"Hah!" the four other male O'Rourkes snorted in unison.

Amidst the laughter, Maddie glanced at Patrick, wondering if she was the only one who saw the darkness in his blue eyes. He smiled at her, yet it didn't reach further than his mouth.

This was the first time they'd been at his mother's house together since the evening he'd reminded her that he wasn't a marrying kind of man. She swallowed the irritation that popped up whenever she thought about it. Talking to her about marriage had been ridiculous when they barely knew each other, and it was insulting to be warned off so quickly.

I want to be honest with you, because your ex-fiancé obviously wasn't.

The memory of Patrick's words tightened her mouth. She didn't care about Ted anymore, and she rarely thought about him except in connection to Patrick. As for being up-front and honest, she couldn't help thinking that Patrick wouldn't have been so anxious to warn her off if she'd been prettier and better endowed. From the bits and pieces of information she'd gleaned from his family, she knew he had a taste for spectacular brunettes with endless legs and salon-toned bodies.

Maddie mouthed a silent curse she never would have spoken aloud. Basically, it didn't matter if a man found you attractive, not when he obviously didn't think you were attractive enough.

She deliberately trained her gaze away from Patrick, only to have it drawn to him again. Restless, she walked over and held out her hand for the container of dressing.

"I think it's mixed enough," she said evenly.

One dark eyebrow lifted. "Don't want to take any chances."

"Right, you don't want to take a chance of being asked to do something else," called Neil, dumping the last of the tomatoes into the salad bowl. "Can't fool me, little brother."

Little?

Maddie's gaze drifted over Patrick. The O'Rourke brothers bore a striking resemblance to one another, and he was equal in size to the others, with a lithe, quick grace that belied his size and strength. She'd felt that strength beneath her fingers, and clenched between her thighs when she'd sat on his lap and learned something about sensual teasing.

He was annoyingly, frustratingly, *gloriously* male, but there was nothing little about Patrick. But it was more than his sex appeal that troubled Maddie's sleep at night, it was his smiles and silences, his intelligence and the frustrating way he kept the world at arm's length.

"Do you have something else?" he asked.

"Something else?" Her tongue flicked unconsciously across her upper lip.

"For me to work on." Patrick swallowed, trying to control the instinctive reaction of his body to Maddie's frank appraisal. He doubted she even knew what she was doing, which made it even more frustrating. He shouldn't be so quick to get hot, particularly in his mother's kitchen, but it was undeniable.

"You can eat it." She took the cruet and started to turn away, but he caught her arm. "What?"

"I just…nothing."

Patrick didn't know what he'd wanted, except for the need to touch Maddie in some small way. It was confusing to have her working at the station, an employee, yet also intimately connected to his family. Every day he was reminded of things he'd rather not think about—of laughter and kisses and the way she'd upset his peaceful world.

He was having more and more trouble staying away from her. Even later, as everyone sat in the backyard bundled in coats and watching the vivid fall sunset, he found himself sitting on the step next to Maddie. She was shivering, still unaccustomed to the damp cold of Washington.

"I'll get you a blanket," he murmured.

Maddie shook her head. "I'm fine."

"Like hell." Telling himself it was the gentlemanly thing to do, Patrick tucked her closely to his side, his arm snug about her slim waist. Except for a small gasp, she didn't protest.

"Dixie has been bugging me to give you a show on the radio," he said after a long moment.

The KLMS audience had not lost their enchantment with Maddie Jackson, and he was running out of excuses why she couldn't go back on the air.

"Doing what?"

"She's calling it the Heart-to-Heart hour. Callers would tell you their romantic troubles, and others would phone in their advice. That sort of thing. It would air in the early afternoon. You'd play some music, and take a few calls in between."

"Oh."

"Any problem with that?"

"I thought you didn't want me on the air. You said I made a mess of it."

He was getting sick of hearing what he'd said. "I also apologized."

"Uh-huh." Maddie stood up and went back into the house.

Sighing, Patrick followed and found her at the door of the playroom his mother kept for his nieces. Amy and Peggy were sound asleep, curled up on oversize pillows. The longing in Maddie's eyes as she watched the twins dragged another sigh from his gut.

"Maddie, don't," he said. "You're only hurting yourself."

"And you're not?"

"We're not starting that again."

She stepped into the hallway. "I'm not a child,"

she whispered. "I know I must seem immature the way I run off at the mouth and don't know squat about men, but I'm a grown woman, and I know what I see."

"I'm aware of that."

"Are you? You keep warning me to stay away, and I'm sure you think it's for my benefit. But you're protecting yourself, not me. You don't want anything to happen that could possibly upset your boxed-up life. Everything else is just an excuse."

"My life isn't boxed up," he denied defensively.

"Yes, it is. I can already hear the hostility in your voice and the warning to stay away—don't get too close, because Patrick O'Rourke won't have it. He knows exactly what he wants, and having to depend on someone else isn't part of the package."

"Wrong," he said tersely. "I don't want anyone depending on *me*. I'm not like my dad—I can't be everything to everybody."

"So you don't even try, because you're afraid you'll fail."

"I know I'd fail." Patrick's jaw hardened. "Look how I've screwed up with you. For once I could do something for Kane by looking out for his wife's sister, instead I've made things worse."

"That's all in your imagination. I don't need to be looked after."

He let out a disbelieving snort. "Like hell. I couldn't keep my hands off you, and you let me do it. What if I hadn't stopped? A lot of guys wouldn't stop after getting that hot and heavy, but you're too innocent to believe it."

"Yes, well, I'm learning fast, aren't I?" Maddie gave a sensuous wriggle of her body, and just that easily he was in trouble. "But I still have to figure out what's real, and what isn't. Maybe I'll go out with a few other men and get some more lessons on living."

Anger and jealousy hit Patrick hard, yet it faded when he looked at Maddie. In the soft light spilling from the twins playroom he saw a single tear trickle down her cheek, evidence of the emotions she was trying to conceal. "You're trying to piss me off," he said.

"Is it working?"

A ghost of a smile curved his mouth. "Yeah, it's working."

Maddie leaned against the wall and closed her eyes. "I don't know why I care."

Patrick rested one hand on the oak paneling above her head and stroked her cheek. "Because you have a big heart and care about everyone."

"So do you."

"No." He shook his head. She was dead wrong about him. He wasn't like her, pulled a thousand different directions by his emotions. It was impossible to undo the harsh lessons he'd received as a teenager.

"You can't keep from getting hurt, no matter how hard you try," she said.

"I can give it a bloody good shot. The world isn't a nice place, Maddie."

"Believe it or not, I already know that—it was difficult to miss when I found Ted with another woman. Or did you think I still wear rosy glasses and think that happily-ever-after is a foregone conclusion?"

"Maybe not foregone, but you still think it's possible."

"Don't you? Don't you think Beth and Kane are

going to make it? Don't you want Neil and Shannon and Kathleen and all your other brothers and sisters to be happy?''

''They're family, of course I want them to be happy. How could you question that?''

''You seem to question it more than I do.''

Weary all of a sudden, he leaned closer to her warmth. Maybe Maddie was right and he was just making excuses. Everything had been calm before she'd arrived, now it was crazy and mixed up, and he couldn't decide if he liked it or wanted the confusion to go away.

''Tell me something,'' Maddie murmured. ''Do you still think I don't know the difference between a great kiss and one that isn't?''

Despite his churning thoughts, he chuckled. ''Are you trying to provoke me again?''

''What if I am?''

Maddie angled her head back. She brushed her lips across Patrick's jaw, and the rasp of his late-afternoon beard shadow made her tummy turn flip-flops. She felt the shudder that went through him, her own body shivering in response.

She'd been so certain she would never get married, never trust a man enough to take that chance. But maybe it wouldn't be such a risk with the right man. Not that Patrick was right for her, but he was so good and decent and sexy she finally understood why women would fling themselves at a guy they barely knew.

''Well, are you going to do something about it?'' she asked, her fingers easing over the broad expanse of his chest.

''Maddie...don't.'' Her name was a cross between

a groan and a plea. Tension stretched his nerves tight as a violin string, drawn by the same old argument between rationality and the demands of his body. "We're in my mother's house."

"And everyone is either outside or asleep."

"The twins could wake up...the others could come back inside," he muttered.

Yet even as Patrick protested, he fumbled along the wall, searching for the doorknob of the closet used to store holiday decorations and seasonal clothing. It was just the sort of dark, private place he needed to kiss Maddie good and hard, then talk some sense into her.

Darkness closed around them as he pulled the door shut, and even sound was muffled by the press of winter coats it was still too early to need. But he hadn't expected to hear Maddie giggle the moment he reached for her again.

"What's so funny?"

"I guess we aren't alone after all. Tiger Lily scooted in with us, she's purring against my leg."

"Tiger Lily can take care of herself."

With unerring accuracy his mouth found hers, and it was such a relief to touch her again the unnatural tension drained out of him. It shouldn't feel so right to sidestep his conscience and give in to his baser instincts.

The cat complained at being ignored, but it was too late. Patrick didn't give a damn how Tiger Lily felt about being locked in a closet with two humans more interested in each other than her royal felininity. And he darned well wasn't going to give Maddie a chance to care.

She felt too good beneath his hands, sweet and eager, mixing sensuality with laughter and honest sexual curiosity.

"How in heaven did you stay a virgin this long?" he breathed.

"Who said I was a virgin?"

He let out a snort. "*I* did, that's who."

Maddie wiggled, freeing one hand and pressing it against his jaw to get some space between them. "You could be wrong."

"No way. Only a virgin would have to ask about this…" Patrick said, rotating his hips, leaving her in no doubt about the hard ridge of his desire. "And few virgins, either. Your boyfriends must have been more gentlemanly than I ever thought of being."

"Ted was my first and only boyfriend, and I think he was too scared of Daddy's gun to try anything," she confessed.

"Gun, huh?" Patrick ran his tongue across her index finger. The muscles in Maddie's abdomen clenched, taken by surprise by the gliding caress. "I'm starting to wonder about that daddy of yours."

"Mmm." She had to take several breaths before her head cleared enough to say something sensible. "There's nothing to wonder about. He used to be the county sheriff. Daddy, that is, not Ted."

"Used to be, eh? Did Daddy get tired of politics?"

"Now he's the mayor."

"Oh."

"I'm sure he didn't actually *threaten* Ted. At least not much," she murmured. "But he can look pretty fierce, and he's very protective."

Patrick was too distracted by feminine curves to answer right away. But if he ever had a daughter, he'd feel the same as Maddie's father. It's what came of being a former bad boy, you knew all the trouble bad boys can make. With his luck he'd have a daughter as wild as he'd been, and there'd be hell to pay.

If he had a daughter?

He hastily stomped on the thought.

"I guess your daddy did what he could, short of locking you up in a nunnery. And that would have been a real waste." Patrick tugged at the hard nub of Maddie's nipple and felt her shudder from head to toe.

She pulled his head back down to her mouth and he tasted the dark, rich taste of chocolate and coffee, with an underlying spice that was Maddie herself. His tongue plunged deeper, exploring her flavors, stroking the velvet softness. This was the way to kiss, slow and deep, wrapped in a cocoon of darkness. No one would ever think of looking for them in the closet, so he had all the time in the world to enjoy the moment.

"We have to talk," he whispered a few minutes later, albeit reluctantly. It wasn't often you found a woman who enjoyed the simple art of kissing the way Maddie seemed to.

"Uh-uh."

"*Now.*"

"Not yet." Maddie spread her fingers across the hot skin of Patrick's back. He was so warm, sleeping with him would be like sleeping with a furnace.

Sleeping with Patrick…she shivered for an entirely different reason than cold. She'd wondered if kissing him would be just as powerful as the first time, but it was even more intense and overwhelming than before.

"*Maddie.*"

She slid her fingers inside his shirt, exploring the

smooth expanse of chest beneath. With a small, desperate sound, Patrick fastened both hands over hers. Both their breathing was erratic, which was small comfort now that he'd apparently decided the kissing was over and the inevitable talking should begin.

"I don't want to talk," she said simply.

"We have to."

"No we don't. We don't have to say another word to each other. You can pretend I don't exist again."

"I never pretended you don't exist."

Maddie straightened her foot and heard a protest from Tiger Lily when she accidentally bumped her nose with her heel. "Sorry, baby," she said. "We're crowding you, aren't we?"

"You don't have to apologize to a cat."

"Why not? They have feelings, too."

If there had been any light in the closet she was certain she'd see Patrick rolling his eyes.

"You're an animal lover, aren't you?" he asked, sounding resigned. "You probably even talk to plants and carry spiders outside so they can go free."

Maddie didn't go quite that far—she killed black widow spiders when absolutely necessary—but she did love animals. Especially cats of any size. They even had a mountain lion who came down to drink at her parents' swimming pool every evening. One time she'd brought her baby, and Maddie had hardly been able to breathe, she was so excited.

"Anything wrong with loving animals?"

"No." Patrick shook his head wryly. She'd managed to effectively sidetrack him. *Again.*

He didn't think Maddie did it consciously, but her clever brain was more than capable of figuring out a way to avoid talking about things she'd rather not discuss. Maddie was a creature of instinct and heart, and she seemed to have her instincts trained on him at the moment.

Only not for marriage, he thought curiously. Maybe not even an affair. Intrigued by sex, yes. Longing for a baby, definitely. But she wasn't a kitten flexing her sexual claws, or a baby-hungry woman on the prowl. She was just…Maddie. Sweet, shimmering with light and possibility, and truly innocent in a way he'd never been, even before losing his father.

The sound of claws pulling on fabric sank slowly into his awareness. A moment later he yelped when something furry and determined dropped on his shoulder and head-butted his temple.

"Where did she come from?"

"The darling." Maddie eased one hand from under his shirt and reached up to pet the little monster. "She must have climbed up the coats. I felt them moving."

Patrick sighed. It seemed Tiger Lily was in cahoots with Maddie, helping her distract him from the important things that needed to be said. Even worse, the stinker was getting more attention now than *he* was.

Women always stuck together.

He opened his mouth only to close it again when he heard someone in the hall, not far from the closet door.

"They're not with the girls," said Kathleen.

"Maybe they went for a walk."

"And I'll bet they didn't want company." Shannon snickered. "No chance any of us might invite ourselves along."

"That was really naughty of you the last time," Kathleen scolded. "You knew Patrick was trying to get Maddie alone."

Patrick winced, knowing Maddie wouldn't appreciate the reminder of their "walk" the last time they'd been at his mother's house together. He'd wanted to talk that night, too, and succeeded in spectacularly stuffing his foot in his mouth. Now he was hiding in the coat closet, trying to keep his family from knowing he'd been necking with a girl.

Maddie was shaking with suppressed laughter, small sounds escaping from her mouth.

"Shh," he hissed.

"Do you feel like you're in high school again?" she whispered.

"More like junior high school, and keep it down. They'll go away in a minute. We can pretend we just came in the side door."

His strategy might have worked if Tiger Lily hadn't decided she'd had enough of the closet.

"Merroowoo."

"Where did *that* come from?" Kathleen said.

Patrick reached up to soothe Tiger Lily back into silence, but the ungrateful little beast sank her teeth into his thumb.

"Ow!"

Tiger Lily dug her claws into his skin for traction when the door was jerked open. She leaped from his shoulder, hitting the floor at a dead run. He instinctively jerked away from the needle-sharp claws and toppled into the thick collection of winter clothing.

He landed on his rear end—which seemed strangely apropos to the situation—barely managing to keep Maddie from the same ignominious collision. Instead she landed on his lap. The breath whooshed out of him, not from her slight weight, but from the contact with his ill-controlled arousal.

Hands parted the various coats and sweaters they'd fallen into, and he gazed up at three of his sisters, two of his brothers and his mother. The topper was when his sleepy-eyed nieces peered at him through the sea of legs.

"I hope you have a good explanation for this, young man," said Pegeen, merriment dancing in her eyes. "I'd hate to have to ground you."

Chapter Nine

"Do you really think so?" Maddie asked. She adjusted the headphones over her ears.

"Absolutely," said the caller. "Trust me, men are pigs."

She giggled. "Richard, you *are* a man."

"Hey, what can I say? Who should know better than one of the swine? My wife says it's genetically linked to the male chromosome."

Patrick sat outside the control booth, watching Maddie charm, laugh and chat her way through her fourth broadcast of Heart-to-Heart. He honestly thought she forgot she was on the air when she was talking to the callers.

"She's wonderful," Dixie said. "So unselfconscious. And the callers just adore her."

"What's not to adore?" he muttered, unable to keep his gaze from Maddie's face.

She had a voice that transmitted well electronically, and she was sweet and sincere. They'd originally planned to play romantic country ballads with Maddie taking a call between the sets—if there were any calls—but talking was crowding out the music, much to the apparent pleasure of everyone tuned in.

For a woman who had every reason to dislike and distrust men, Maddie was as generous and open with the male callers as she was with the women. At the moment she was earnestly trying to convince Richard, and Richard's wife, that being a man didn't automatically condemn a guy to swine-like behavior.

Patrick sat back in his chair, shaking his head.

A secret concern he'd harbored about the show was that it would be one of those sappy, syrupy things that slowly began to grate on your nerves. To Dixie's credit, she'd created an introduction and format that was as straightforward and unpretentious as Maddie herself.

"Didn't I tell you this would work?" Dixie asked, gleefully rubbing her hands together. She was in her element as the producer of not one but two successful programs.

"I never said it wouldn't," he reminded.

"But you didn't want her to do a show."

He gave Dixie a repressive look. "Maddie has a mouth that runs away with itself faster than light speed. You never know what's going to come out."

The producer ducked her head to answer one of the incoming calls, but not before Patrick saw her grin. He didn't blame her. By now everyone in the station had decided that he and Maddie were involved in some way. It was a huge source of amusement and jokes, though entirely out of Maddie's earshot.

Thank goodness.

Crockett was a small town, but it was close enough

to Seattle that most everyone had a veneer of city sophistication. His employees seemed to understand Maddie was different and saved their raised eyebrows and comments for him alone.

At least they didn't know about the coat closet.

Though he'd expected to wince each time he thought about getting caught with Maddie, it hadn't worked out that way. All in all, it had been rather funny. Two grown people caught necking like a couple of kids. There hadn't been any doubt about their activity, not with his shirt hanging out and Maddie's face and neck showing a faint case of whisker burn.

Now Patrick understood why Kane had begun shaving so often, he didn't want to irritate his wife's delicate skin—skin that was just like Maddie's.

In another few minutes Dixie signaled to Maddie that time was nearly up. They'd learned to schedule extra minutes for the wrap-up since Maddie wouldn't hurry people off the phone because she claimed it was rude. If time was left over they just played a song until the next DJ took over.

The Seattle Kid, fully recovered from his bout with the flu, already waited inside the booth. Mack wore a paternal look on his face as he helped Maddie start a song, gently encouraging in a way the wisecracking DJ had probably never acted in his life.

"The audience isn't the only one who thinks she's great," Dixie said, smiling.

"You're just grateful he didn't take your head off for getting his show shortened."

"Naw, his audience is even bigger now 'cause they're all hoping she'll come back on again."

Maddie came out a minute later. "Was that all right?" she asked the producer, a hint of anxiety in her voice. He noticed she didn't so much as flick an eyelash in his direction. It stung, although he should have been grateful she was trying to keep things on a professional level, at the station at least.

"You did great," Dixie said. "Don't forget we're returning your rental tonight and picking up the car from your sister."

Patrick frowned. "What?"

"Beth is loaning me her Honda to save money on the rental," Maddie explained. "But the car place is at the Seatac Airport and I need a ride back. Beth wanted to go, but she doesn't have a lot of energy right now because of her pregnancy. Kane didn't want to leave her alone, and I didn't want him hiring someone to do it, so Dixie offered to help."

"You could have asked me."

Maddie's feet shifted uneasily. "I didn't want to inconvenience you."

"It isn't inconvenient," he said through his teeth. "I'll take you myself."

"But you aren't—"

"Whatever you say, boss," Dixie said, cutting off Maddie's protest. She gave him a broad wink that was meant to be funny, but Patrick didn't think it was the least bit humorous that Maddie hadn't wanted to ask him for a simple favor.

It was no big deal to go to the airport and bring her back. He'd wanted things uncomplicated, but that didn't mean he was living on a desert island or anything.

Hell, even his family hardly ever asked...

Time stretched endlessly as some hard truths sank into Patrick. His family was always careful not to ask more than he wanted to give, which apparently wasn't much from their perspective. The only thing his mother pushed about was coming to family dinner, and even then she was gentle and undemanding.

No guilt.

Just concern.

What he didn't know is whether they felt they *couldn't* count on him or were just giving him the distance he wanted.

Patrick ran his hand over his suddenly aching head. Maddie said he put up barriers between himself and the family. He'd denied it, but what if she was right? He didn't want to deal with pain and confusion, so he just walled it away, outside his heart…along with everyone else.

"I'd better get back to my desk," Maddie said. She was silently backing into the corridor as if getting ready to run.

"No. We'll go for the car now."

"I have work to do."

"You're a DJ now, and your show is over."

"But Stephen needs—"

"Stephen is getting all the help he needs from Candy," he interrupted harshly.

God, he'd been right about Maddie turning his life upside down. She'd put the station on its ear, upset the familiar order of things by getting her own show, plotting a romance between his stern receptionist and advertising director, and making him question his relationship with the entire world.

"We're going now," he said, grabbing Maddie's arm and dragging her toward the door. It would probably take the entire drive to Seattle—Maddie in her rental and him in the Blazer—to get his head back together. Maybe they should take the long way around through Tacoma, avoiding the ferry, then he'd have more time.

"You're mad," she said, trying to shake free.

"No, I'm not."

"It's all right. I'll just keep the rental until Beth feels better."

He stopped and sighed. "I don't mind helping out. I have a lot on my mind, that's all."

Maddie could relate to that, she had a lot on her mind, too. Namely Patrick. He was the most frustrating, annoying, *wonderful* man she could imagine, and no matter how often she told herself they didn't have a future together, she'd spent a lot of time daydreaming in the past few days.

Dumb. Just plain nuts. Patrick might own a country music station, but he wasn't going to fall for a country girl.

She tucked a stray strand of hair behind her ear. Leaving in the middle of the day smacked of special privileges from the station owner, but she wasn't going to bring it up at this late date.

"I need my purse and the keys if we're going into the city. I left them in the office."

Patrick chuckled ruefully. "A little hard to drive without keys. Go ahead, I'll wait outside."

Maddie hurried to her desk, her heart thumping loudly. His smile tended to disturb the steady rhythm of her pulse, and today was no exception. Willing herself to calm down, she picked up the phone and dialed her sister's number. It was the polite thing to do and would buy her a little time.

"Beth? It's me," she said when her twin answered. "We'll be there earlier than I thought. Patrick wants to go to the airport now, instead of waiting until this evening."

"I thought someone else was bringing you."

"No." Maddie craned her head to see if Stephen was at his desk. She'd been so distracted she hadn't even looked before. Thankfully, he was gone for the moment. "Patrick insisted."

"That's interesting."

"Uh, Beth, about that thing with the closet. You know he…that is, we aren't dating or anything. But he's been very…uh, I don't know how to describe it."

"Attentive?"

"Not exactly. It's more like trying to get acquainted with a yo-yo."

"Patrick has had some tough times, but he's a really good person," Beth said earnestly. "Kane is so proud of him. And even though he'd like to help out, he respects how independent Patrick wants to be."

"It's more than being independent."

"I know, but he'll come around. Don't give up on him."

Maddie swallowed. "There isn't anything to give up on. Patrick has made it very clear he isn't a marrying kind of man and he doesn't want children. He keeps warning me not to get ideas about us. And I'm not his type," she added.

Her sister didn't say anything for a long minute. "I wasn't Kane's type, either. Now he thinks I'm perfect. I'm not, but he makes me feel that way."

"You've had two men in love with you," Maddie said. "My fiancé cheated, then admitted he never really loved me, and Patrick has a thing for svelte brunettes."

"Bet you could make him forget all about those brunettes."

"You'd lose. Look, he's waiting for me, so I'd better go. See you later."

Maddie put the receiver down and pressed her palms against her eyes. Her trip to Washington hadn't turned out the way she expected. It was satisfying to know she was good at her job. It was terrific having a sister; she and Beth were getting closer every day. She loved the O'Rourkes and the fact that Pegeen was trying to mother her, even though she had a wonderful mom of her own.

But Patrick…

He frustrated her so much she wanted to scream. There was such a wonderful guy inside him, a man perfect to be a husband and daddy. But no, he wanted to be free and single, standing square on his own two feet and needing no one else.

She'd never met such a mouthwatering man. His brothers were attractive, but Patrick had a mix of laughter and raw sexuality that was positively breathtaking. In all honesty she couldn't blame Patrick for wanting someone who was prettier and more experienced, but the part she found so hard to take was that he didn't want to want her. He even resented the extent to which he did find her attractive.

A hand on the back of her neck made her jerk upright. But it wasn't Stephen with his warm, sympathetic eyes looking at her, it was Patrick.

"I'm sorry, I meant to come right out."

He leaned on the edge of the desk. "Maybe we *should* wait if you have a headache."

"It's nothing. I was delayed because I called Beth to let her know we'd get there early."

"I should have thought of that."

"It was my responsibility." She took her purse from the drawer and fished out the keys. "I'm ready when you are."

"Maddie." He paused and seemed to search for words. "I appreciate you taking on the new show. It's really popular, which doesn't happen very often."

"I like talking to people."

"That's why it works. You just talk without trying to be clever at the cost of the caller's feelings. People know you care about them."

She opened her mouth, then shut it just as quickly. They *weren't* going to get into another discussion that tore at them both. She cared about people, he thought he was immune from those feelings. He wanted to be alone, satisfied with his radio station, she wanted… everything.

Love with the right person wasn't a myth or impossible or anything else. It was worth the risk of a broken heart, even a broken soul. She knew that now. But crying because Patrick refused to understand wouldn't help either one of them. Neither would talking about it.

"I'm ready," she said, standing. She automatically reached for her jacket, and just as automatically Patrick took the garment and helped her into it.

His old-fashioned manners were as deeply ingrained as the air he breathed. Too bad some old fashioned commitment wasn't mixed in with those manners. It wasn't as if he was a wolf, dating a different woman every night. Apparently Patrick wasn't dating anyone at the moment. His entire focus seemed to be on his business and making it the number-one country music station in the state.

"Would you prefer following me?" he murmured as they stepped outside. It was a beautiful day filled with the colors of leaves turned yellow and bronze. "I won't let you lose me."

"Sure."

Maddie started her car and waited. Patrick probably knew the way to the airport far better than she did and would negotiate the freeways and ferry without the consternation she would feel.

He did everything well.

Everything except let someone love him.

The following week Patrick decided he didn't need to sit in the control booth and monitor Maddie's broadcasts, mostly because it made him ache to listen to her.

In some strange way it seemed she was slipping away from him. He saw her just as much and could see her even more, but the feeling had more to do with the guardedness of her smiles and the way her mouth didn't run away with itself when they were together. There were a dozen subtle changes in the way Maddie responded to him, though she was herself with everyone else.

There was a knock on the door and Patrick sighed. Never a moment to think in the radio business. If it wasn't one thing, it was another.

"Come in," he called out.

Stephen nudged the door open and wrestled his wheelchair into the closet-like space.

"You need a bigger office," he said.

"We all do." Patrick waved his hand dismissively. He'd taken the smallest room in the station as his office, because he wouldn't ask his employers to take less than he would himself.

Stephen smiled. "The ad office space works better now that Maddie rearranged everything. She's certainly a multitalented young lady."

Maddie.

Patrick tried to keep his face impassive. Maddie had insinuated herself into every part of the station, every part of his thoughts and life. And she'd done it unknowingly, because she didn't have a calculating bone in her body. The only time her innocent fire was subdued was when they were in the same room. The other employees and his family must have noticed, though no one had said anything.

"I know it's inconvenient having her do the show. I'll look into getting more help in advertising," he said.

"She's keeping things up. Maddie has a rare gift with people—we're selling more airtime than ever before."

Oh, yes. Between Maddie's new program and her honest approach, they were practically at the point of turning advertisers away. Air rates had gone up, especially during her show, and revenues were pouring into the KLMS bank account.

"I know Maddie was supposed to be temporary, but have you discussed a long-term contract with her?" Stephen asked. "It would be a shame to let her return to New Mexico in a week…when Jeff returns."

Patrick stared at his friend. Time had passed so quickly that he'd forgotten Maddie was temporary, and that the employee she'd replaced was coming back to work shortly.

Hell, they'd launched her new show without a single thought of what would happen when her temporary employment terminated. And he couldn't even claim he'd believed Heart-to-Heart would flop, because deep down he'd known the rest of the world would find her nearly as irresistible as he did.

"I'll start thinking about it," he muttered. "But there's no need for her to leave right away. She can stay on, helping out wherever she's needed."

"Good. In the meantime, I wanted to tell you…" Stephen paused, showing a rare moment of indecision.

"Yes?"

"Well, lately I've been spending quite a bit of time with Candace Finney. I've always known she was a special lady, and the long and short of it is that I've asked Candy to marry me," the older man said.

It was the last thing Patrick had expected to hear. "You have?"

"Yes." Stephen smiled, clearly pleased. "I might have courted her years ago, but I knew she was nursing an invalid mother and I didn't think she'd be interested in a man in a wheelchair. Especially before her mother passed."

"It would have been her loss," Patrick said quietly.

He meant it. Stephen Traver was strong and fit, with a keen eye for human nature. The accident that put him in a wheelchair might have happened when he was in his early twenties, but no one could ever make the mistake of thinking he was helpless. Courting the Formidable Finn was probably the only thing he hadn't done, including sky diving.

Stephen was living proof that when bad things happen they didn't have to ruin or control your life.

As the sense of his thoughts sank in, Patrick winced. He might have had a great example of courage and fortitude to follow, but he hadn't learned much from it.

"I hope you'll both be happy," he said sincerely. "You deserve it."

"So do you."

Patrick looked sharply at Stephen, but could read nothing in the other man's expression.

"That's a matter of opinion," he murmured.

"Your opinion, your life—your decision."

"I made that decision a long time ago."

Stephen's eyes were grave now, and he shook his head. "And what about Maddie?"

"Maddie…" Patrick set his jaw. Everyone believed they were having an affair, but he'd be damned if he'd explain that nothing had really happened between them, even to his friend. "I'm not like my father. I can't be everything to everybody."

"He wasn't anything of the kind. In fact, you're still pissed that he failed."

Patrick shoved away from the desk, furious. "My father never failed at anything."

"He failed the worst way a father can fail," Stephen said, looking oddly pleased. "It was the ultimate failure. He died. When you needed him the most, he was dead. And you've never forgiven him for it. Isn't it about time you let it go?"

"You don't know what in hell you're talking about," Patrick snarled.

Sure, he'd been angry about his father's death, but dying wasn't Keenan O'Rourke's fault. It had been an accident, pure and simple.

Just then the blue light alarm on his desk rang

sharply, startling both of them. For a fraction of a section Patrick stared at the blinking light. He'd installed it as a precaution, a few days after buying the station from C. D. Dugan—a way for the Formidable Finn to alert him of trouble at the front desk. Until now it had never been used.

With an agility that testified to his powerful shoulders and arms, Stephen maneuvered his wheelchair aside far enough for Patrick to get out the door.

Patrick hit the corridor running, only slowing a few feet before turning the corner into the lobby. He didn't know what he'd find, maybe an upset client or listener, or a thief who didn't know the station didn't keep money on the premises. The possibilities were endless and it didn't pay to burst into the situation, making it worse.

"Gosh, you must really like to sing."

It was Maddie's voice, and Patrick's heartbeat stopped for a long moment, then jumped into triple digits.

"Yeah…yeah, and you haven't played a single demo I've sent."

Demo?

Patrick thought about the hundreds of demo tapes sent to KLMS by aspiring songwriters and singers. Most of them were pure junk, desperate dreams of the untalented. Very rarely they found a gem in the bunch and played it, giving full credit to the artist.

He stepped slowly, noiselessly, into the small lobby and saw something that hit him like a sledgehammer—Maddie, her arm held in a tight grip by a young man with stringy hair and a hard set to his profile.

"What kind of songs do you write?" Maddie

asked. She sounded friendly and interested, the way she did on the radio. Yet Patrick could see her wince as her arm was jerked.

"Rock and roll. Great rock and roll, not that this pissant station would know the difference." He sounded even younger than Patrick had originally thought.

"Oh. No wonder we didn't play your songs," she said, making it sound as if the answer was so logical and understandable that even a maniac could understand.

A maniac...Patrick had trouble drawing air into his chest. An angry listener was one thing, an unhinged singer-songwriter was another. He eased farther into the lobby, ready to tackle them both if necessary. The one thing in his favor was that he wasn't in the guy's direct line of sight. The bad part was that he couldn't see if a knife or gun was involved.

The thought of deadly force being pointed at Maddie made ice run through his veins.

"What do you mean?" snarled the intruder.

"We're a country music station now. It used to be rock and roll, but we changed. Haven't you heard our motto? 'KLMS, we're *your* country music.'"

"Maddie, that's 'We're KLMS, your station for country music,'" Candace Finney advised. She'd acknowledged Patrick with a slight flicker of her eyes, but not enough to alert the intruder.

"I always mess it up. Actually," Maddie said in a confiding tone, "we have a lot of mottoes, like not having dead air on the radio and being the prize-winningest station, but all radio stations are probably the same. I don't know, what do you think?"

The guy seemed distracted. "About what?"

"Radio. I don't know very much about it. My name is Maddie, and you're...?"

He blinked and shook his head. "Scott Dell, but my band's name is the Puget Busters. You're that girl who comes on in the afternoon, Heart-something-or-other, aren't you?"

Patrick could tell the man's grip had eased on Maddie's arm, but he didn't seem ready to let go anytime soon. Actually, he could hardly be called a man. He looked to be in his mid-teens, with low-riding jeans and feet too big for his lanky body.

"Hey, I'm not a girl," Maddie said, exasperation in her voice.

"Yes, you are." Patrick took a step forward as if he'd just arrived and everything was calm and normal.

"Patrick—"

"Maddie," he mimicked back. "You're a girl, we're guys, and we don't know why it's such a big deal."

"My girlfriend says it patronizing," said the teenager.

She gave them both a narrow look. "It's the difference between being a child and being an adult. Would you like it if I called you a boy?"

Patrick didn't feel the least bit like bonding with the youngster still keeping Maddie prisoner, but his gaze met the intruder's, and they both shrugged.

"Men," she fumed. "How about if I call you 'nice.'" I bet *that's* a different story, isn't it?"

"There's nice and there's nice," Patrick said.

"Yeah." The kid nodded. "Nice is all right."

"If you're a puppy dog," Patrick qualified.

Scott laughed and dropped Maddie's arm. With a

clear view of both his hands, no weapons, and no bulges in his pockets, Patrick immediately put himself between the two of them.

"Go back to work," he ordered over his shoulder.

"But, Patr—"

"*Now,* Maddie."

"Uh…it was nice meeting you, Scott," she said as she turned and headed for the back of the station. "The boss says I have to go back to work now. Work can really take the fun out of a day."

"It's better than not having any," Scott muttered, looking both sad and angry.

Patrick waited until Maddie was out of sight, then fixed the teenager with a stern eye. His first urge was to throttle the kid, but he knew what it was like to be young and angry, and how important second chances could be.

"What in hell were you thinking, young man?" Jeez, he sounded just like C. D. Dugan the night he'd been caught trying to hotwire the truck.

Scott kicked the ground with a sulky foot. "No one will play my songs."

"How old are you?"

"Nineteen."

Patrick lifted an eyebrow and waited.

"All right." The kid's shoulders slumped. "Fourteen. But they're good songs and I gotta make some money. Mom is sick and Dad can't…" His words trailed miserably.

Through the double glass doors Patrick saw a patrol car pull into the lot, but he held up his hand when the officers got out. The men nodded and waited.

"Your father is out of work," Patrick guessed.

"Man, everyone says the economy is great, but he can't even get an interview."

"I know that's rough, but you broke the law coming in here like this. You know that, don't you, Scott?"

"I guess."

Around the corner Maddie waited with almost everyone else in the station. From Stephen she'd learned that Patrick often worked with troubled youth, something she could have guessed from his sympathetic yet firm tone of voice.

Within a few minutes Scott was sitting in the back of the squad car, with one of the deputies promising to call his parents. A deal might be worked out with juvenile court considering the circumstances.

And Patrick, who wouldn't take a red cent from his brother for his own needs, promised to call Kane and get Scott's father a job.

Maddie's throat closed around quick tears.

She'd tried so hard not to fall in love with him, but she couldn't deny it any longer. Patrick O'Rourke had her heart in his hands, and he didn't want it.

Chapter Ten

Maddie barely had time to form the thought before she heard one of the deputies say he needed to speak with her. She groaned. She didn't want to say anything bad about Scott; he was just a mixed-up kid with more troubles than he knew how to handle.

When Patrick rounded the corner with the officer he cleared his throat and gave a pointed look to the assembled employees.

"Show's over," he said.

They drifted away with obvious reluctance.

"Ms. Jackson." The officer, Deputy Walter Mitchell, nodded at her, then looked down at his notebook. "Can you tell me what happened?"

Maddie slipped her arm behind her back. "I was in the lobby talking to Candy. Scott came in and wanted to know why we hadn't played any of the demo tapes he'd sent the station. He didn't know we only play country music, not rock and roll."

"And...?"

"And that's about it."

"No, it isn't," Patrick said patiently. "Maddie, Scott has to take responsibility for what happened. He was out of control when he grabbed your arm. Anything could have happened."

"May I see your arm, Ms. Jackson?" asked the officer.

She reluctantly pulled it from behind her back.

Patrick clenched his jaw at the bruises already forming on Maddie's skin. The imprint of rough fingers were perfectly aligned across her forearm.

"Damn kid, I should have *killed* him." He knew he was overreacting, but everything was different with Maddie. Too big, too vital, too much a reminder of how much he had to lose. The speed at which she'd become important to him sent shock waves through his system.

"I bruise really easy," she said. "It's nothing."

Deputy Mitchell wrote some notes on his pad. "Do you want to file assault charges, Ms. Jackson?"

"No."

"Yes," said Patrick. "Maddie—"

"He's just a scared kid," she interrupted. "With a lot of problems. He didn't mean to hurt anyone."

"That's an excuse, not a reason."

The deputy measured the compassionate look on Maddie's face and the outraged thrust of Patrick's jaw.

He tapped his pencil on the pad. "We checked. The kid doesn't have any priors. Never been in trouble, period. We'll make him look at Ms. Jackson's arm, then I'll put the fear of God into him about doing anything like it again. If he keeps his nose clean, there won't be any charges filed. If he doesn't, he gets an assault rap on his juvenile record.''

Patrick counted to ten, trying to calm down. He couldn't remember the last time he'd been so furious. But it wasn't just anger at Scott Dell, it was at himself. He should have had security measures in place from the very beginning, but instead he'd let a wild-eyed kid come in and hurt Maddie. It could just as easily have been a real maniac, and Walter Mitchell could have been completing his report over her dead body.

Maddie hastily agreed to the officer's suggestion and followed him out to the squad car.

When Scott saw the bruises he paled. ''I didn't mean…oh, man. I'm sorry. I never meant to do that, I just wanted someone to listen.''

''I know, it isn't—''

''It doesn't matter what you intended,'' Officer Mitchell said, cutting off Maddie's reassurance. ''Now, we're going back to the station to have a nice long talk. Do you know what the jail sentence is for assault and battery? I do, and you're going to hear all about what happens to young punks in prisons. It isn't pretty.''

Scott gulped and huddled deeper into his seat. Maddie gave him an encouraging look, but he was too scared to acknowledge it.

Over the roof of the car, the deputy winked at Maddie.

After they left, she spun around and glared at Patrick. ''Why did you have to make such a big deal out of it?''

''You've got bruises all over your arm. What did you expect me to do?''

"Help him. You're still going to get his father a job, aren't you?"

Patrick let out a harsh breath. "If he's lucky."

"You said you would."

"Stop telling me what I said!" he shouted.

"You blew it all out of proportion."

"I asked you to work at the station and put you at risk. What's out of proportion about it?"

She rolled her eyes. "That's a bunch of nonsense."

"No. I'll never be able to take care of you the way I should. That's why I can't get married—I'll mess up. I always mess up. I won't be there when you really need me, and then everything will go to hell."

Maddie's jaw dropped. Patrick was serious about that "take care" of her stuff. He'd said it before, but she'd thought it was just male ego talking.

Take care of her…hah! It was the most insulting thing he'd ever said. Just because she'd run away from the humiliation of her canceled wedding didn't mean she was incapable of dealing with life. Hadn't she been trying to prove that? Working at the station and being good at it? And she *had* been doing well; he couldn't deny it.

"You aren't responsible for what just happened, and I do *not* need someone to take care of me," she said fiercely.

"You're a baby."

"No, I'm not. I'm a grown woman."

This wasn't a word game any longer, it was dead serious. She'd never intended to get her heart tangled up with Patrick, but it had happened, it wasn't going away, and she had a dismal conviction that this time she was going to find out what a broken heart really felt like.

"I've done things you can't even imagine."

"I've got a great imagination," Maddie said. "But I don't need one. My father wasn't always the sheriff or town mayor, he used to be a roughneck, determined to prove he was more than a kid from the wilds of New Mexico who happened to get lucky with a football. And he's been very honest with me about his mistakes."

"You're not making any sense." Patrick jammed his hands into his coat pockets. The last traces of easygoing humor had been erased from his eyes and mouth.

"Dad won a football scholarship, but his teammates called it dumb luck. They didn't believe someone could come from a school with barely enough students to *form* a football team could have any talent. No matter how good he was, he had to prove it to them over and over. So Daddy decided he was going to be the meanest, nastiest one of them all."

Patrick was intrigued despite himself. "And?"

"And that's what he was, until he met my mother."

"Right, true love solves everything." He tried to sound mocking, but it was never love Patrick hadn't believed in. It was the agony and loss he didn't want. Nobody had to tell him love was real, he'd seen how much his parents loved each other, and now it was the same with Kane and Beth.

Love and passion were real.

So was the pain.

"Don't worry, I'm not hoping for history to repeat itself," Maddie muttered. "You're already reformed, so if I *was* interested in a bad boy, I'd look somewhere else. Never mind that I wasn't looking at all," she added quickly.

He sighed. "Fine, but I know what I was. Nothing can change the fact that I'm experienced and you're not."

Maddie rolled her eyes. Patrick meant sexual experience more than anything else. "There's a simple solution," she said in a suggestive voice. "Picking up a guy at the local bar is easy. After that I'll just let nature take its course."

From Patrick's outraged expression she knew she'd struck a nerve.

"Don't even joke about it."

"Who's joking?"

"You are, damn it. You aren't the type to go sleeping around."

"How would you know?"

"A man knows things like that."

He was pure, unadulterated arrogance, and if she hadn't loved him so much she would have been disgusted. As it was, she was bothered more than she should have been about Patrick's insinuation that she couldn't take care of herself.

"But you must admit it would be easy. Unless you've been lying about me being attractive."

"I'd never lie to you. Of course you're attractive. A guy would be crazy not to take you home, but that's not the point."

"It's exactly the point," Maddie snapped. "The kind of experience you're talking about is easy to get. And it's just one part of life, not the whole package."

"Fine. It's easy. But you don't have any experience with anything."

"No? I live in a small town where everybody

knows everybody else's business. Do you think I haven't seen and heard the worst there is to see? My uncle was run over by a drunk hit-and-run driver who turned out to be a cousin. Uncle Julio won't ever walk again, and the cousin spent eighteen months in jail. Two years ago I was on a search team looking for a lost Cessna in the Magdalenas. We found the plane, but it was too late for the pilot." Her voice wavered, though she tried to keep it level.

"Maddie, *don't.*"

Patrick felt as if he were being flayed alive. They could trade scars until they were both bruised and beaten by the memories, but it wouldn't change a thing. She was too special, too sweet and too damned tempting. Sooner or later she'd figure out he wasn't good enough for her and leave.

"You come from a little town no one has ever heard of, Maddie. I know real life happens there, but it isn't like the city. People in towns that small *do* know other people's business and take care of each other."

"I didn't realize Crockett, Washington, was the hot spot of metropolitan life," Maddie said sarcastically. "Where I come from isn't the issue, and you darn well know it."

"I'm not just from Crockett..." Patrick stopped. This wasn't getting them anywhere. "You're right, the place we're from isn't the issue any more than you being a virgin. Aside from the fact you don't have a clue how to take care of yourself outside of Slapshot," he couldn't resist adding.

"So you still think someone has to take care of me?"

"Yes, and I'm not the one to do it," he snarled.

"You said it yourself, I'm not involved with the family in a way that really matters. No one counts on me for anything. I'm the brother who screws up, it's as simple as that."

"Don't be ridiculous." Maddie looked him up and down, her chin jutting out the way it did when she was being particularly stubborn. "You may have messed up as a kid, but you can't keep blaming yourself for it. You were at a hard age, and you were angry with your father for dying. Everyone understands that except you."

It was the second time in less than a day that someone had suggested he was angry with Keenan O'Rourke for the mere fact of dying. Oh, Patrick knew about the so-called stages of grief, and that anger was a natural part of them, but there was no way he was angry with his dad. It just wasn't true.

Or was it?

Was the reason he couldn't see himself stepping into his father's shoes because deep down he believed his dad had failed him? And if Keenan O'Rourke could fail, what hope did his screw-up son have to succeed?

Maddie looked at him narrowly, obviously expecting him to say something. When he didn't, she shook her head.

"You're one of the most successful people I know," she said. "You thought of the 'billionaire date' promotion and made it work. You've taken a barely functioning radio station and turned it into one of the most popular stations in the area. You're a responsible businessman. You work with troubled teens and make a difference in their lives. Nobody could ask more of a person, except to let go of the past.''

"Maddie—"

"And you're a darn good kisser," she shouted. "Everything else is an excuse."

"I don't need an excuse."

"Hah."

But even Maddie's skepticism couldn't stem the pleasure flooding through him. She thought he was successful, despite everything she'd learned about his past, and a tight knot of pain eased inside of Patrick. For all of Maddie's apparent flightiness, she was smart, sincere and had solid values. She was the kind of woman whose opinion mattered.

"You really think I'm successful?"

"I don't say things I don't mean. And it was obvious the way you talked to Scott that you've got a gift with kids. But don't get all defensive," Maddie said quickly. "I'm still not asking you to be a daddy."

"Because you don't think I'd make a good one?"

"No, because you don't want to *be* one. I know the drill perfectly—you've taught it to me well enough. Stay back, don't get too close, and don't start getting ideas. But you'd better start telling yourself that, because you're the one with all the ideas. Most of them completely idiotic. 'Take care' of me...give me a break.''

Maddie turned and stalked back into the station, her back straight as a board.

Patrick cursed and sagged against the nearest car. He'd overreacted, handling things so badly it was a wonder Maddie hadn't slugged him. But hell, those bruises on her arm were enough to give him nightmares. She'd said he wasn't responsible, but he *felt* responsible. He wanted to keep every single possible danger away from her.

Now you're thinking, son.

The voice.

Patrick pressed the heels of his hands into his eyes. At least he was lucky enough to remember his father's voice. It wasn't true of his youngest sister, barely four when Keenan died. Kathleen had only vague images of a laughing man she'd worshipped, of strong arms and a comforting presence. But no voice, no memory of life lessons taught by a patient, wise, loving man. At least the older kids had that much.

Jeez, he missed his father. Still missed him, with nearly the same aching grief he'd known in the weeks and months after the accident.

Maddie reminded him of the principles Keenan had taught him. Principles like being honorable. Lessons about what made a boy a man. And ducking responsibility because he might get hurt or fail wasn't one of those lessons. You couldn't always prevent disasters or keep the people you cared about from harm.

Showing up was what counted.

There were a thousand clichés to describe the way he'd been living his life, but it all boiled down to being just a spectator. The radio station didn't count for anything—that was just about money.

Real living was about loving, and he'd done his best not to love for the better part of twenty years.

"Your son is the most stubborn, unreasonable, hardheaded man ever born," Maddie stormed.

She dropped down on Pegeen's couch and glared at the picture of Patrick that hung on the opposite wall. He was so appealing with that killer O'Rourke smile and hidden pain behind his eyes. It made her ache to see it and know he wasn't ever going to change. At the same time she was furious because he couldn't see truth standing right in front of him.

Love wasn't the enemy; it was the solution.

"He's impossible," she added, a litany of even less attractive descriptions running through her mind—some were words she would never dream of saying aloud.

"I can't deny it, darlin'," Pegeen said in her lilting Irish brogue. "He's the way nature made him."

"Nature has a lot to answer for," Maddie grumbled.

She didn't know why she'd come to see Patrick's mother, but it had seemed like a good idea at the time. Pegeen was a lovely woman who shared the same comforting quality as her own mother. And since Pegeen knew her son, she'd understand the frustrations he visited on friend and foe alike.

Darn him.

She didn't need to be taken care of. She was managing fine. All his nonsense over the incident with Scott Dell was just a way of reminding her they didn't have a future together.

Take care of her...

Maddie gritted her teeth. How you could love a man so much and still want to strangle him was a mystery she'd never understand.

"He makes it sound like a man would have to be a superhero to risk marrying me," she muttered. "And he...he has this thing about not being 'like' his father. As if he's the black sheep of the family, or something. I know he made mistakes, but who doesn't?

Your husband must have been a great man, but Patrick doesn't have to be exactly like him to be a good husband and father. Nobody wrote *that* into the rule book, did they?''

Pegeen sat next to her and took her hand. ''Actually, of all my sons, Patrick is the most like his father.''

Surprised, Maddie tore her gaze from the photograph. ''He is? Why doesn't he know that?''

The older woman lifted her shoulders in a shrug. ''He was young when we lost Keenan, still lookin' up to his father but not much knowin' him. But they have the same heart, fierce and gentle and proud as a man comes. And his laugh…it's like hearin' Keenan all over again.''

''Stubborn?''

''Oh, yes. Keenan was a terror as a lad. M'parents didn't want me to have anything to do with him, but a girl in love doesn't listen overwell. We courted until I told him plain I wouldn't have a troublemaker for a husband. He'd have to mend his ways or find another woman to make his wife.''

''So he changed.''

''Ah, no.'' Pegeen let out a warm chuckle. ''Not right away. It was hard for him, bein' in the same town where he'd caused so much ruckus. That's one reason we came to America. A clean start for us both.''

''I see.'' Maddie thought about the way Patrick commanded respect at the radio station, his lively wit and intelligence making everyone forget the troublesome boy he'd once been. Keenan had made a measured choice to start over with his family; Patrick had chosen to stay and make his way in a world that knew his secrets and failings. Both were difficult choices, but neither one of them had run away.

Her first instinct after fighting with Patrick had been to leave immediately. But she wasn't going to run away, either. Leaving the scene of her ruined wedding was one thing, running away from her job and responsibilities was another. She'd finish her time at the radio station—there were just a few days left until Stephen's assistant got back—then she'd leave a forwarding address and return to Slapshot.

Patrick would be able to find her.

If he ever wanted to know where she'd gone.

"Will you come back to Washington for the wedding?" Candy asked as she hugged Maddie goodbye. "And be my maid of honor?"

"I'll try."

"Maybe we could get married in Slapshot," Stephen suggested.

A smile broke through Candy's tears and she smiled at her fiancé. "That's a wonderful idea."

Stephen neatly tugged Candy across his legs and handed her a handkerchief. "Who'd have guessed?" he said good-naturedly, taking his bride-to-be's tears in stride.

"Oh, you." Candy sniffed and gave him a kiss guaranteed to notch his temperature up a few degrees.

Maddie tried to not envy them. They deserved to be happy. Candy had even confided they were going to try to have a baby. The doctor had advised it would be a high-risk pregnancy, given Candy's age, but not impossible.

"You'll never know how much you've meant to

us," Stephen said quietly. "I only wish you and Patrick…" He shrugged and didn't finish the thought.

"I know." Maddie couldn't resist glancing around, hoping Patrick would show up. She'd asked her new friends not to make a big deal of her leaving. Nevertheless, they'd thrown an impromptu party with snacks and sodas from the vending machines. It would have been nice if Patrick had shown up, if only to say goodbye.

Of course, they'd probably just have another fight.

"You can't leave," Dixie moaned for the thousandth time. "What about the show? It's such a big success. Everyone is going to be so upset."

"I was only supposed to be here temporarily."

"But Patrick never said you were leaving."

"That's right, I never did."

The low masculine voice sent flutters through Maddie's tummy. She spun around to see Patrick regarding her with a long, unsmiling stare. He even looked angry—as if *he* had a right to be upset after the irritating things he'd said the last time they'd spoken.

"Would everyone leave us alone?" he asked.

The assembly of KLMS employees hastily headed for the break room door. All except Stephen, who had reluctantly allowed Candy to scramble from his lap. "Just don't be a jackass," he said to Patrick.

"I don't recall asking for your advice."

"When has that stopped me?"

A reluctant smile tugged at Patrick's mouth. "Never. But I don't have to listen."

It was a routine they'd gone through in the early years, when Patrick had been still rebellious and angry and reluctant to listen to anyone. In fact, he usually did listen to Stephen, but the news that Maddie was leaving had hit him like a ton of bricks. He'd hardly been able to breathe, much less think clearly.

He'd assumed Maddie wouldn't leave unless he told her to go. No wonder there'd been so many subtle and not-so-subtle hints about offering her a contract to do her show. Nobody wanted to lose her.

The whole station adored Maddie.

And damn it, he did, too.

Stephen wheeled out the door, then closed it behind him.

Patrick drew a rough breath, then looked at Maddie. "You don't have to go. I would have told you if I wanted that."

"How big of you. You sound so thrilled with the idea, too. About as excited as you were when you hired me. You regretted it, didn't you?"

"That's beside the point," Patrick said, not bothering to deny it. He *had* regretted hiring Maddie, but it wasn't because of who she was as a person or her value as a worker, it was the way she'd made him feel. A man didn't enjoy feeling vulnerable, and that's exactly what she'd done to him.

Her chin rose. "Now you can have things exactly how you want them. You don't have to worry about having to 'take care' of me. I won't be around. And I'll make sure you don't have to see me any more than necessary. Maybe Kane and Beth can come to New Mexico to visit after the baby arrives, instead of the other way around. Then you won't have to be inflicted with me at all."

"That isn't what I want," Patrick said harshly.

"Yes, it is."

"No, it isn't," he insisted. "Just stay in Washington while we figure things out."

Maddie shook her head, her eyes stark and dry without her usual quick tears. "It won't change anything."

Panic crowded his usually sensible brain. He couldn't let her leave, he just *couldn't*. "All right, fine, I'll marry you," he snapped.

Hell.

It didn't take a crystal ball to know he'd just made a huge mistake. Maddie gave a look like he was gum she needed to scrape off her shoe, and he heard a collective groan from outside of the room—where, no doubt, everyone in the station had gathered to hear his business.

He tried to ease the tension in his shoulders while thinking of a way to repair the damage. Women wanted flowers and romantic declarations of love, not shouted proposals of desperation.

"I didn't…quite mean it that way," he said carefully.

"I'm sure you didn't mean it all."

"I meant the part about marrying you."

Maddie sighed. Just getting married wasn't what she wanted, she wanted a partnership like her parents had, a passionate, endless love that defied all the rational reasons why two people shouldn't be together. She finally knew why Patrick's notion of taking "care" of her bothered her so much. She'd already had one blow to her self-confidence; she didn't need another.

She shook her head. "No."

"Look, I'm sorry about the way I said it. I'm an idiot. I've messed up all along where you're concerned, why should it be any different now?"

Maddie looked at him, seeing a man she loved but

also someone who couldn't trust himself, much less anyone else. "*I'm* different."

"What's that supposed to mean?"

"It means I won't let anyone make me feel inadequate again. No matter how scatterbrained and emotional I might be, I'd make a darned good wife. I don't need to be taken care of, I need to be loved and trusted and made a partner. But you can't do that, because you're so hung up on the past you can't see the future."

"That isn't true. And I never meant to make you feel inadequate. You aren't, I just..." He threw up his hands. "I just need some time. I really care about you, can't you see that?"

"I see more than you think."

Maddie swallowed around the tight knot in her throat. He liked her, he just didn't want to like her too much. He didn't want to like *anyone* too much. The hardest part about loving Patrick was knowing that it wasn't just her he wouldn't let into his heart, it was the entire world.

"If you weren't so worried about who is going to take care of whom, and being so blamed independent, you might figure out what families and love are all about," Maddie said. "And maybe then you'll stop protecting yourself and let someone else inside. Until then, I'll be in New Mexico."

She turned and very quietly walked out the door.

Chapter Eleven

Patrick rested his fists on his thighs. He'd proposed, been turned down, and he still didn't quite believe it.

The irony of spending his life avoiding commitment only to be refused by the one woman he really wanted to marry wasn't lost on him. He'd probably even laugh about it in fifty or sixty years.

"Oh, man," he muttered to himself. "Why couldn't you have gotten smart faster?"

It had been foolish to assume that just because he wanted to get married, Maddie would, too. She didn't have any reason to think he'd changed.

I won't let any man make me feel inadequate again.

Hell. Why had he insisted she needed someone to take care of her? Her innocence was a precious, wonderful thing, but it didn't make her incapable. It was his own inadequacy he'd feared.

A man was supposed to protect his woman— whether she needed it or not. His sisters called it a macho, old-fashioned attitude, but he didn't care.

There were a lot of things he might be able to change about himself, but that wasn't one of them. If he accepted responsibility as a husband, he'd damn well do it the way it was supposed to be done. Not that Maddie couldn't do some taking care of him, as well; he wouldn't mind some tender loving attention from her.

All the time, he really *had* been protecting himself, not Maddie. He'd known she was a generous, loving woman who wouldn't care about the stupid things he'd done as a teenager. He'd just been afraid to break out of the shell he'd built around himself to wall out possible pain. So he'd spend nearly twenty years alone, even though he was surrounded by people who loved him.

That's why he'd envied his brother and Beth. They had something he'd been afraid to find for himself.

Without needing to look up, he knew Stephen had returned, probably wearing the stern expression that meant he was in for a lecture. "Go ahead and say it," he muttered.

"I just wondered what you're going to do now?"

"What do you think?" Patrick retorted. "I'm getting a ring and propose the proper way."

"Bring a few dozen roses to go along with that proposal," Stephen advised. "She's pretty steamed."

"Any particular color?"

"I think you can figure that out on your own."

There was no condemnation on Stephen's face, only concern. Even now Patrick didn't know why Stephen Traver and C. D. Dugan had cared enough to straighten out a hell-bent teenager, and he'd certainly never publicly acknowledged the favor.

"Have I ever thanked you for bailing me out of trouble more times than I can count?" he asked.

"Yes, by making something of yourself. Now go finish the job and marry Maddie."

"Aye, aye, sir." Patrick gave him a mock salute, but the real acknowledgment was silent. They weren't the kind of men who said things easily between them.

Hell, he hadn't even said the most important thing to Maddie…that he loved her. Struck by the thought, Patrick kicked himself all over again.

I really care about you.

What an insipid thing to declare to the woman you loved more than your own soul. No wonder she'd walked out on him. She had her pride, too, and would never be the first to admit she loved him after the way he'd acted.

And she did love him. He knew it with a certainty that defied reason. She belonged to him in the way men and women have belonged to each other since the beginning of time.

Patrick went first to Maddie's desk, only to find Jeff Tarbell sitting at it.

"Need something, boss?"

"Where's Maddie?"

"Gone. She cleaned out her stuff last night. Say, she's really something. Do you know she organized the entire—"

Patrick didn't hear the rest. He was already running out the door, his heart in his throat. Maddie might belong to him, but where was she?

He dialed the bed-and-breakfast inn on his cell phone, only to learn she'd already checked out.

"Damned woman. She's *too* efficient," he muttered.

He climbed into the Blazer. Maybe he could catch her at the airport. He wouldn't have a ring, but he could get flowers from a vendor. Except, he didn't know what airline Maddie was flying on or anything else.

Beth.

If anyone would know, it was Beth. Patrick tried reaching his sister-in-law at her clothing store, then caught her at home. "Beth, where is Maddie?" he demanded when she answered.

"Patrick...I don't think she wants to see you."

"She's there?" Hope rose in his chest as he turned the Blazer toward his brother's place.

"No. She didn't want to fly, so I suggested she drive back to New Mexico. I'm not using the car, so it seemed the best solution. We said goodbye before she went into work this morning. I thought you knew she was leaving."

Patrick ground his foot on the brakes, screeching to a stop. "She's *driving?*"

"She's an excellent driver," Beth rebuked gently. "She does a lot of off-road driving in New Mexico, and we made sure the car was fully inspected and equipped."

"But it's snowing in Utah and across the pass in Oregon," Patrick said, trying not to yell. "Which way is she going?"

"I don't know. She said she hadn't made up her mind."

He struck his forehead against the steering wheel. It would be days before he could see Maddie. And if she got stuck in the snow it might be even longer. He wanted to chase after her, except that would only convince her more than ever that he didn't respect her ability to take care of herself.

At least he could be there when she arrived.

''Uh...is Kane around?'' he asked. ''I'd like to borrow the company jet.''

Three days of driving hadn't helped Maddie's aching heart, but it had been better than dealing with the hustle and bustle of the airport and crowding herself onto an airplane. She'd never driven such long distances before, and there was a certain kind of calm in the passage of the miles and the impersonal sterility of motel rooms.

Slapshot didn't look different when she descended the highway down into town. The little church where she was supposed to have been married still stood in the middle of the block. The Hamburger Shack had the same cars in front of it, and the air smelled of piñon pine and the lingering fragrance of roasting chilies.

Home, and yet not home.

Not any longer.

Her home was with Patrick O'Rourke, even if she never saw him again. As it turned out, love really was that simple. Sometimes your heart made choices your head couldn't argue over.

It was an unusually warm fall day, and she rolled the window down as she pulled into her parents' driveway. They would probably be out by the pool, savoring the last reminder of summer. Leaving her suitcases behind, Maddie walked through the house and onto the patio beyond. Her dad was working with the hose, spraying off the natural-rock paving stones around the pool, while her mom worked on the terraced flower beds.

"Guess who?" she called.

Her father's face split in a grin as he strode forward and grabbed her into a huge bear hug. "Baby, we thought you wouldn't be here until tomorrow."

"I got up especially early. I wanted to get home." Her throat was choked with tears as her mother joined the hugging and kissing. "I missed you so much," Maddie whispered.

"Did you miss *me?*" asked a familiar voice.

For a moment it felt as if the ground had dropped away from her feet. It couldn't be Patrick. Not in New Mexico. Not standing right behind her.

"Don't I get a kiss, too?" the husky voice added.

Swallowing, Maddie turned and saw Patrick regarding her with solemn blue eyes. What was he doing here? She needed peace and quiet, a place to gather herself. She didn't want another fight; she had to be strong and not let him talk her into something that would be wrong for them both.

"How…" She cleared her throat.

"I got here Friday evening. Your parents and I have been getting to know each other."

"Friday? But how could you… The airlines couldn't get you here so quickly."

"Mmm, no. I borrowed Kane's company jet. Turns out the Slapshot airfield is big enough to land in. I could have slept on the plane with the pilot, but your mom and dad offered to put me up while I waited to see you."

"They did?" A traitorous warmth crept through Maddie. Patrick must have wanted to get to New

Mexico really fast to ask for something so expensive from his brother.

Susan Jackson smiled serenely. "I think barbecued chicken would be good for dinner. We'd better get it started, Hugh."

Maddie's father kissed her forehead. "Welcome home, baby. We missed you." He followed his wife into the house.

"Baby?" Patrick lifted one eyebrow. "You let him get away with that?"

"Fathers are allowed," Maddie said.

Patrick smiled. He liked the Jacksons. They were a passionately devoted couple who reminded him of the way his own mother and father had loved each other. He'd spent the past three days talking with them, being frank about his mistakes. And he'd discovered the same nonjudgmental quality in them as he'd found in Maddie.

The past was the past.

What mattered was what you did with your future. He could only pray that Maddie would have enough forgiveness in her sweet heart to give him another chance.

"I'm not afraid of your father or his gun, but we'd better get married fast, because I don't want our first child born less than nine months after the wedding."

Maddie drew a quick breath at Patrick's happy, utterly wicked grin. "Oh, yeah? I thought you didn't want to have children—no more changing dirty diapers or reading *Mother Goose*. Remember?"

"That was before I fell in love," he said quietly. "Now I want everything. If you have enough love and faith in me to be my wife, then I'll make darn sure not to mess it up."

When she didn't say anything, Patrick sighed.

"Sweetheart, I can't help being protective, but it has nothing to do with how wonderful I think you are. A man wants to protect the woman he loves, and all the logic in the world won't change that. Your father is the same, but do you really believe he thinks less of you and your mother because of it?"

"No."

"Please, Maddie," he urged, stepping so close she felt the warmth radiating from his body. "I'm tired of being alone. You can't leave me like this, not when you've shown me what can be. I *love* you."

Unable to resist his plea, Maddie threw herself into Patrick's arms. "And I love you," she whispered against his lips.

"Does this mean you'll marry me?"

She gave him that saucy, impudent smile he adored. "What do you think?"

Patrick caught sight of the Jacksons peering out from the kitchen window. From behind Maddie's back he gave them a thumbs-up. "I think you should stick your hand in my back pocket," he murmured.

"What?"

"Just do it."

The sensation of slender fingers sliding into his jeans' pocket nearly brought Patrick to his knees. "Get all three of them," he growled. "And fast, or your father is going to be very unhappy with me."

"I thought you weren't afraid of Daddy."

"*Maddie.*"

"You…*oh.*" Tears spiked Maddie's eyelashes as she looked at the three rings lying on her palm. Two engraved wedding bands, one obviously for a man, and a beautiful channel set diamond and sapphire engagement ring.

"I know it's traditional to pick out the wedding bands together, but I hoped you wouldn't mind. Especially since your mom helped." He slipped the engagement ring over the third finger of her left hand.

She drew back with a serious expression on her face. "All right, I'll marry you," she said. "Just so long as you know, I don't believe in long engagements."

Patrick drew his thumb across Maddie's lip. "You're going to have the shortest engagement in Slapshot history. Your mom promised she could put together a wedding in two days, and I sent the jet to Washington so it could bring everyone back here. Provided you agreed to marry me, of course."

"Of course," she said, and kissed him back.

Four Weeks Later

"That feels so good," Patrick said, groaning at the ache in his muscles.

"That's what you get for trying to inspect the transmitter in the middle of a thunderstorm," Maddie said gently, rubbing liniment into his back and shoulders as he lay sprawled across their bed.

Despite his aches and pains, Patrick smiled into the pillow. His wife was sweet and wonderful, but she wasn't shy about saying "I told you so."

Maddie had scolded furiously when he'd climbed onto the platform to check it out after the worst of the storm passed, declaring that someone else who was better qualified could do it later. But nobody knew that old transmitter the way he did, and he'd wanted to be certain it was okay after the wind they'd had.

"It was perfectly safe. The storm was almost over," he said.

"No, it wasn't. It's still pouring down rain. If it was 'almost over' it would have stopped by now."

Patrick chuckled, turning over to smile at her. "This is winter in Washington. It's basically going to rain for the next six months. That's what keeps it—"

"Green," she finished for him. "I know."

His grin faded as he traced the line of Maddie's face. She was so lovely, so passionate about everything. She brought the same enthusiasm to their marriage that she brought to everything else. Still, maybe asking her to adjust to the weather in the Pacific Northwest wasn't fair.

"We could move," he said quietly. "We could start a radio station in Albuquerque, or I could do something else."

Maddie blinked. "Why would we want to do that?"

His shoulders lifted in a small shrug. "Some people have trouble getting used to the short winter days and rain up here."

"Have I complained?"

"No."

"Then stop worrying about it. I like the rain." She bent over him, giving a long kiss that sent Patrick's pulse racing. "Except when you insist on climbing all over a transmitter in the middle of a storm."

"But you miss your parents," he said hoarsely.

"Luckily I have your mother, my sister, and the rest of the O'Rourkes to help when I get homesick. And you haven't seen our first long-distance phone bill.'' Maddie's fingers were busy unsnapping the buttons on his worn jeans.

Patrick helped her maneuver the jeans down his legs. He kicked them out of the way. ''I don't give a damn about the bill,'' he growled. ''I just care about getting you naked.''

''Oh, yeah?''

Maddie sat back on her heels and admired her husband's powerful body. They probably would have made love in the Blazer if she hadn't been shivering so hard when they left the station. They most certainly would have made love taking a warm shower, but Patrick had gotten a call from Pegeen…much to his sexual frustration. He'd left the bathroom, pulling on the jeans and ordering her not to put on any clothing herself, but she donned a T-shirt and panties for comfort.

''What?'' His eyebrows shot upward. ''You'll give me a massage, but you won't get naked for me?

Maddie smiled and slowly lifted the hem of the T-shirt. ''Are you sure you don't mind about the phone bill?''

Patrick snorted. ''Give me a break.''

She tossed the shirt to one side and focused on Patrick. She loved to see his pupils dilate when she got ''naked'' for him. A woman couldn't ask for a more passionate, lusty husband. He didn't have *any* inhibitions in the bedroom and had rapidly demolished any she might have had.

''What are you thinking?'' Patrick asked as Maddie crawled over him like a sensuous cat.

''That you took care of my inhibitions.''

''Huh. As if you had any.'' He nuzzled the space between her breasts, then kissed his way to the velvety tip. Breath hissed through Maddie's lips, making him smile. She was an enthusiastic lover, with the same natural talent in making love that she had in kissing. "Are you sure you're happy here?" he asked, a lingering concern in the back of his mind.

Maddie sat back, her bottom landing on his unprotected arousal. He groaned at the exquisite pain.

"Will you stop that?" she demanded. "I'm an adult. If I was unhappy I'd tell you."

Well, hell. He wasn't going to argue with that logic.

He pulled her down beside him. "Fine. But *I'm* a little unhappy you're still wearing these." Patrick hooked his fingers around her panties and tugged. Maddie obliged by digging her heels into the mattress and lifting her hips. He tossed the panties over his shoulder. "You're very helpful."

Maddie's smile was sultry as she ran the curve of her foot down his leg. "I don't want my husband to be unhappy."

"There's not a chance of that."

Oh, man, she really did have the prettiest breasts. Patrick swirled his tongue over one nipple, teasing the other with his fingers.

Maddie squirmed, the muscles in her abdomen clenching and grabbing in the most delicious way. Most of the time it was slow and hot between them, but she didn't want that tonight. She needed him fast and hard and *now*. It had frightened her, seeing Patrick working on the transmitter, wet and exposed, lightning forking across the sky. He was probably right that he hadn't been in danger, but fear wasn't logical. Shuddering, she muttered a sensual demand and felt him jerk.

It was like setting off a nuclear bomb, sensations igniting, rolling over her with a power that still left her filled with breathless astonishment, no matter how many times they'd made love in the past weeks.

The lightning from the storm was nothing compared to the electricity in her veins. She tried to wait, but her body exploded, sending her into a shimmering, mindless void of pleasure.

With a final gasping thrust, Patrick fell into the same void, collapsing over Maddie. With the last of his energy, he rolled, tucking her along his side so his greater weight wouldn't crush her.

Nearly twenty minutes passed before he lifted his head. Maddie had a sleepy, satisfied smile he loved knowing he'd put there.

"Don't look smug," she murmured.

"I'm not smug, I'm happy."

"Okay."

Patrick settled back, hardly able to believe the difference she'd made in his life. Not just the greatest sex ever, but warmth and love and acceptance.

Kane and Beth had insisted Maddie and Patrick buy Beth's old house at a ridiculously low price. The house was in excellent condition and would be a perfect home for them, at least until they had more than a couple of kids. They could remodel later, or get something bigger if that's what they decided.

A thoughtful frown creased Patrick's brow as he remembered Maddie's reaction—or rather, lack of reaction—when her period had come on schedule. She'd wanted a baby so badly he was surprised she'd taken it so calmly.

"Sweetheart, about a baby…"

"It's all right," Maddie said quickly. "I don't

mind if we wait. I've been thinking I should go on birth control for a while.''

The sated lassitude in his body vanished. "Why?"

"You know, to give y—*us* some time before starting a family.''

Damn. He looked at her in exasperation. "You mean give 'me' some time. I don't need time. We can have a baby now.''

"Well, not *right* now," Maddie said, glancing down at her flat tummy.

"Maddie." Patrick lifted himself on one elbow and looked down at his wife. "What's going on?"

"I just don't want you to think the only thing I wanted…" She rubbed her hand on his arm. "You're more important to me than having a baby.''

A burst of warmth surrounded Patrick's heart, and he blinked rapidly. Modern men might be comfortable enough to cry, but he wasn't that modern.

"I already know that," he said, stroking her face. He should have shaved, there was already a blooming case of whisker burn in several sensitive places—like her cheeks and breasts. "And a baby is something we both want.''

Maddie smiled tremulously. "Are you sure?"

"Positive." Patrick kissed the red marks he'd left on her skin. She shivered, her nipples tightening in instant response. "And since making a baby is so much fun, we win two ways.''

Maddie arched her neck, the familiar tension flooding back through her body. "Sounds…like a plan.''

"Mmm, I love amenable women.''

"Patrick O'Rourke, that's not what—"

His hand swooped over her mouth, cutting off her words.

"Just checking to be sure you were listening." Patrick grinned as he lifted his hand. "You get distracted so easily."

Maddie found a particularly responsive place on her husband's body and noticed he was a little distracted himself.

"You were saying?"

"Not a thing," he breathed.

"I thought so." She pulled him down, her fingers threading through his dark hair. "Now make me forget I married a man who climbs out on radio transmitters in the middle of storms."

"Delighted to oblige."

Patrick's kiss deepened as he did exactly that.

* * * * *

Reader favorite

PATRICIA THAYER

continues her popular miniseries,
The Texas Brotherhood, for

SILHOUETTE *Romance*®

Don't miss the next story in this exciting family saga:

Jared's Texas Homecoming

(SR #1680)
Available August 2003

In this powerful romance,
a rugged loner searches for
the truth about his past and
meets a single mother who
shows him the meaning of
family...and true love.

THE TEXAS BROTHERHOOD
continues in February
and March 2004
with two more
page-turning romances!

Available at your favorite retail outlet.

Silhouette®
Where love comes alive™

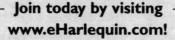

If you enjoyed what you just read,
then we've got an offer you can't resist!

Take 2 bestselling love stories FREE!

Plus get a FREE surprise gift!

Clip this page and mail it to Silhouette Reader Service™

IN U.S.A.
3010 Walden Ave.
P.O. Box 1867
Buffalo, N.Y. 14240-1867

IN CANADA
P.O. Box 609
Fort Erie, Ontario
L2A 5X3

YES! Please send me 2 free Silhouette Romance® novels and my free surprise gift. After receiving them, if I don't wish to receive anymore, I can return the shipping statement marked cancel. If I don't cancel, I will receive 6 brand-new novels every month, before they're available in stores! In the U.S.A., bill me at the bargain price of $3.34 plus 25¢ shipping and handling per book and applicable sales tax, if any*. In Canada, bill me at the bargain price of $3.80 plus 25¢ shipping and handling per book and applicable taxes**. That's the complete price and a savings of at least 10% off the cover prices—what a great deal! I understand that accepting the 2 free books and gift places me under no obligation ever to buy any books. I can always return a shipment and cancel at any time. Even if I never buy another book from Silhouette, the 2 free books and gift are mine to keep forever.

215 SDN DNUM
315 SDN DNUN

Name	(PLEASE PRINT)	
Address	Apt.#	
City	State/Prov.	Zip/Postal Code

* Terms and prices subject to change without notice. Sales tax applicable in N.Y.
** Canadian residents will be charged applicable provincial taxes and GST.
All orders subject to approval. Offer limited to one per household and not valid to current Silhouette Romance® subscribers.
® are registered trademarks of Harlequin Books S.A., used under license.

SROM02

©1998 Harlequin Enterprises Limited